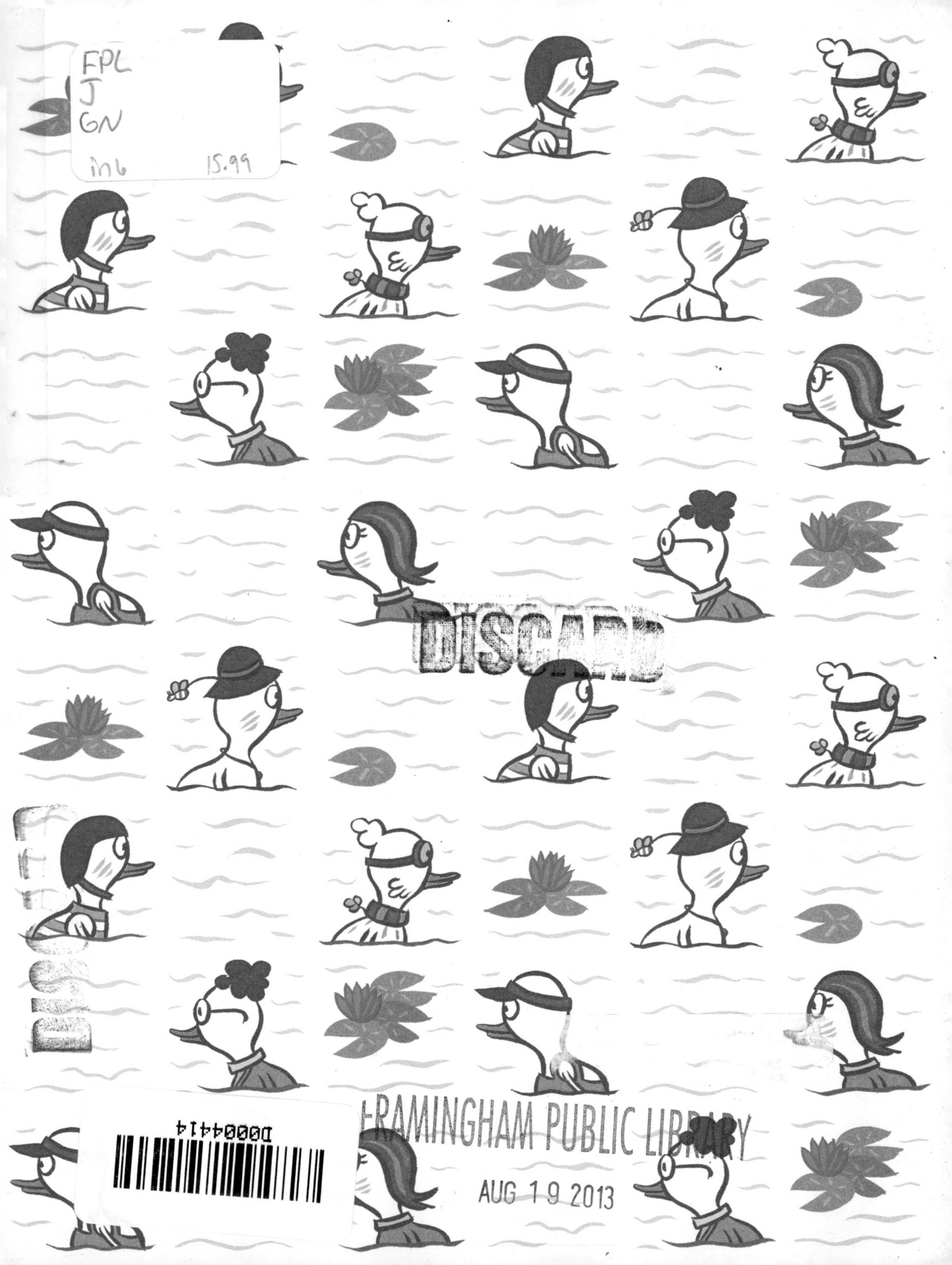

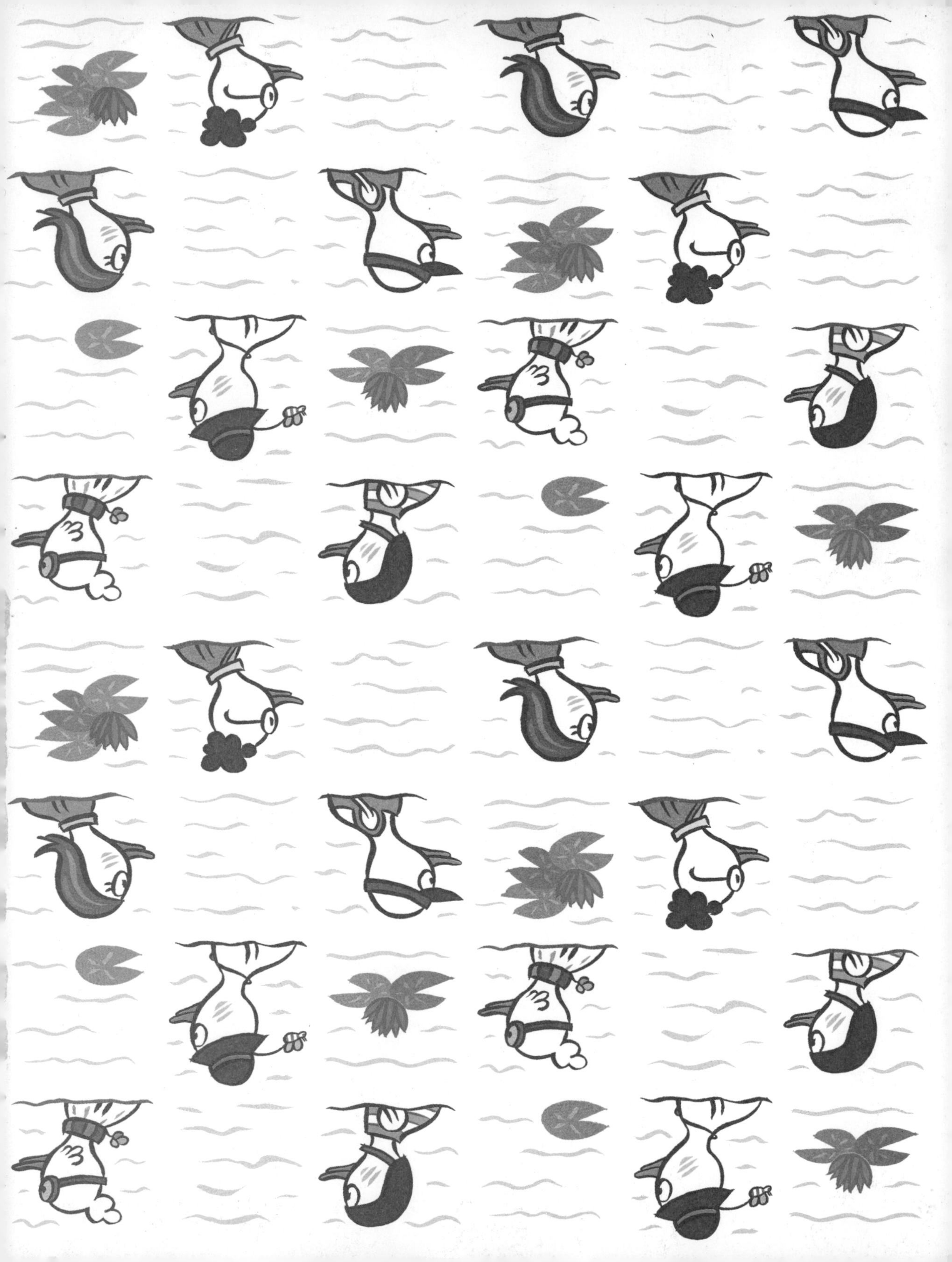

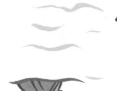

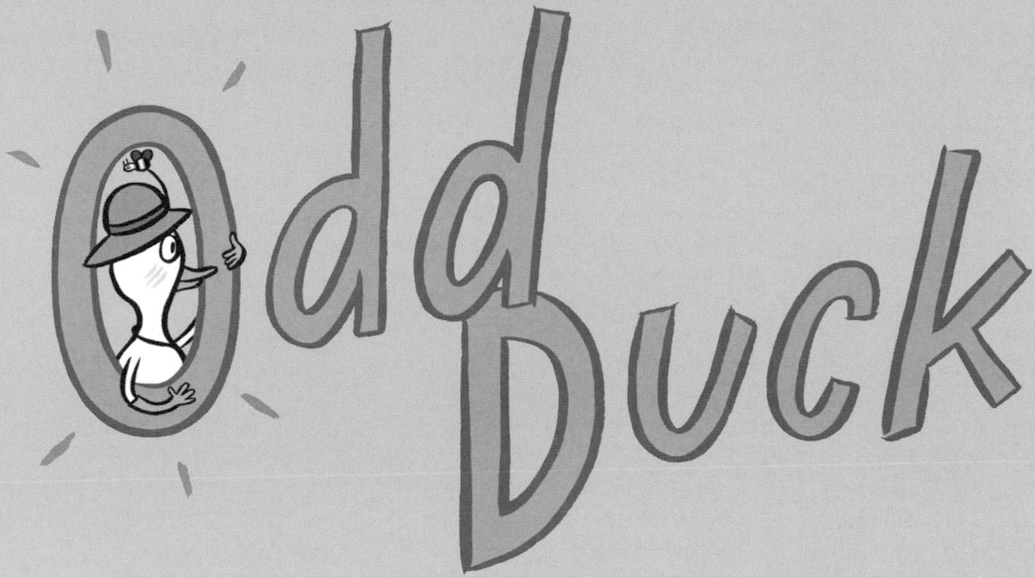
Odd Duck

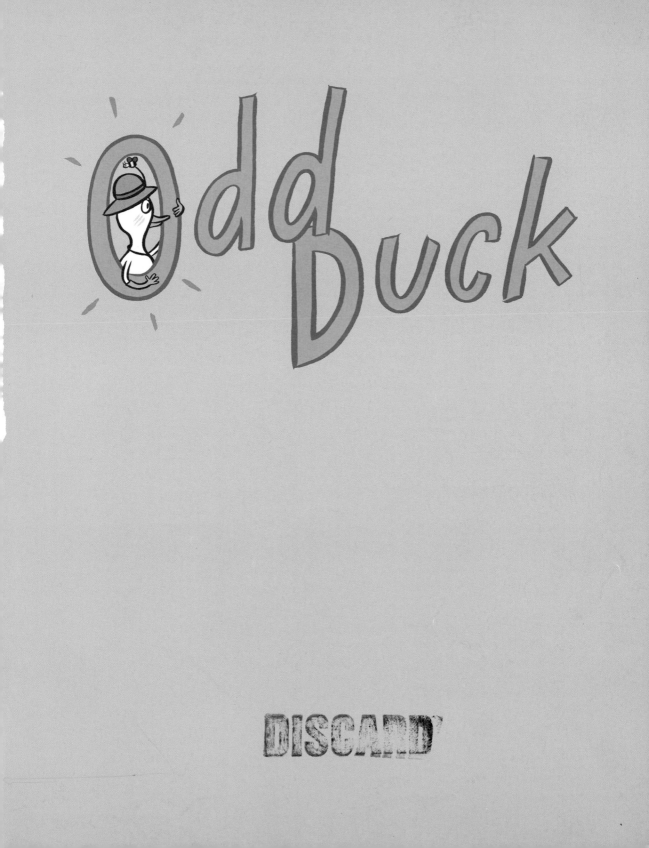

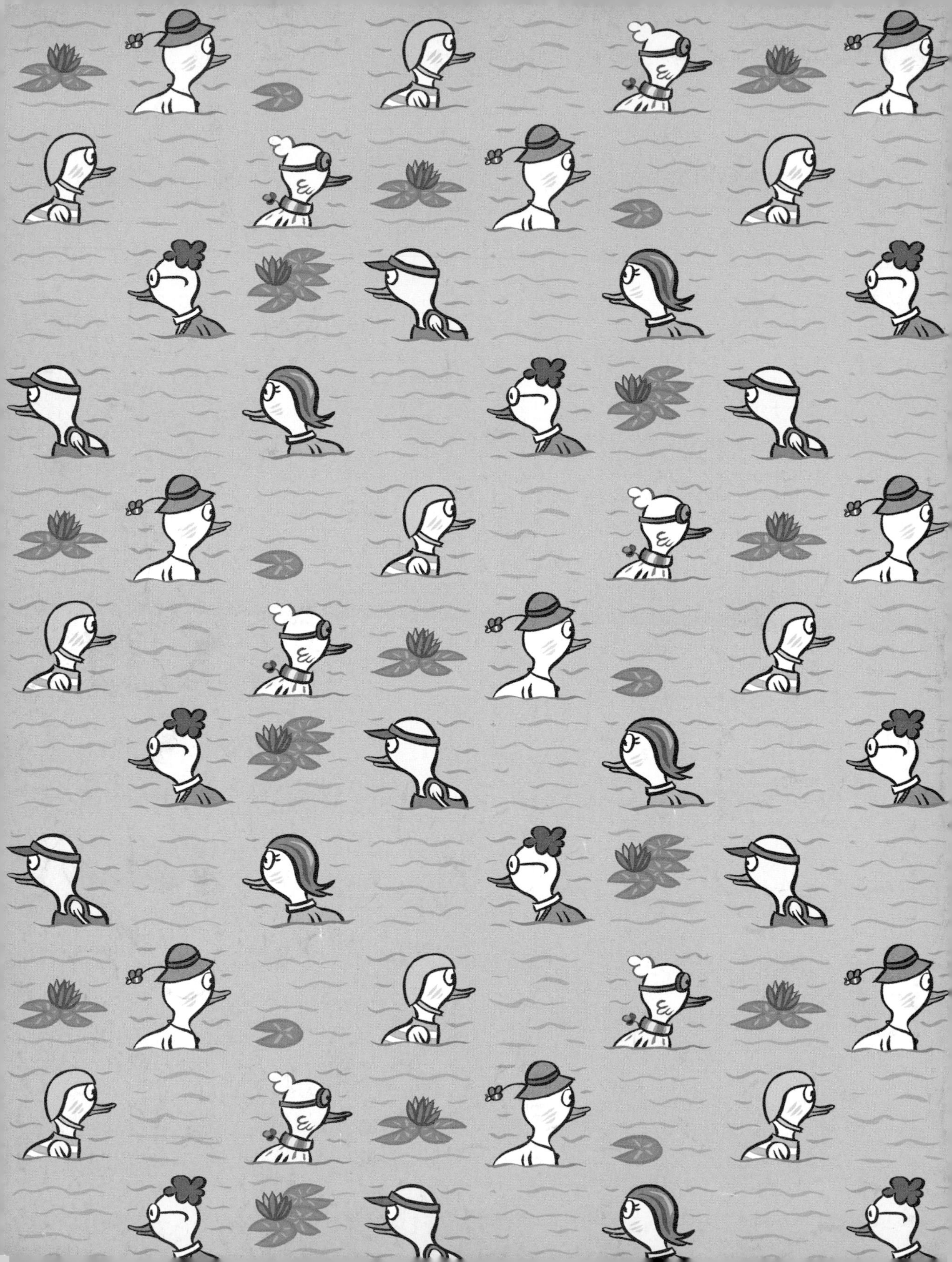

Odd Duck

Cecil Castellucci
& Sara Varon

First Second
New York

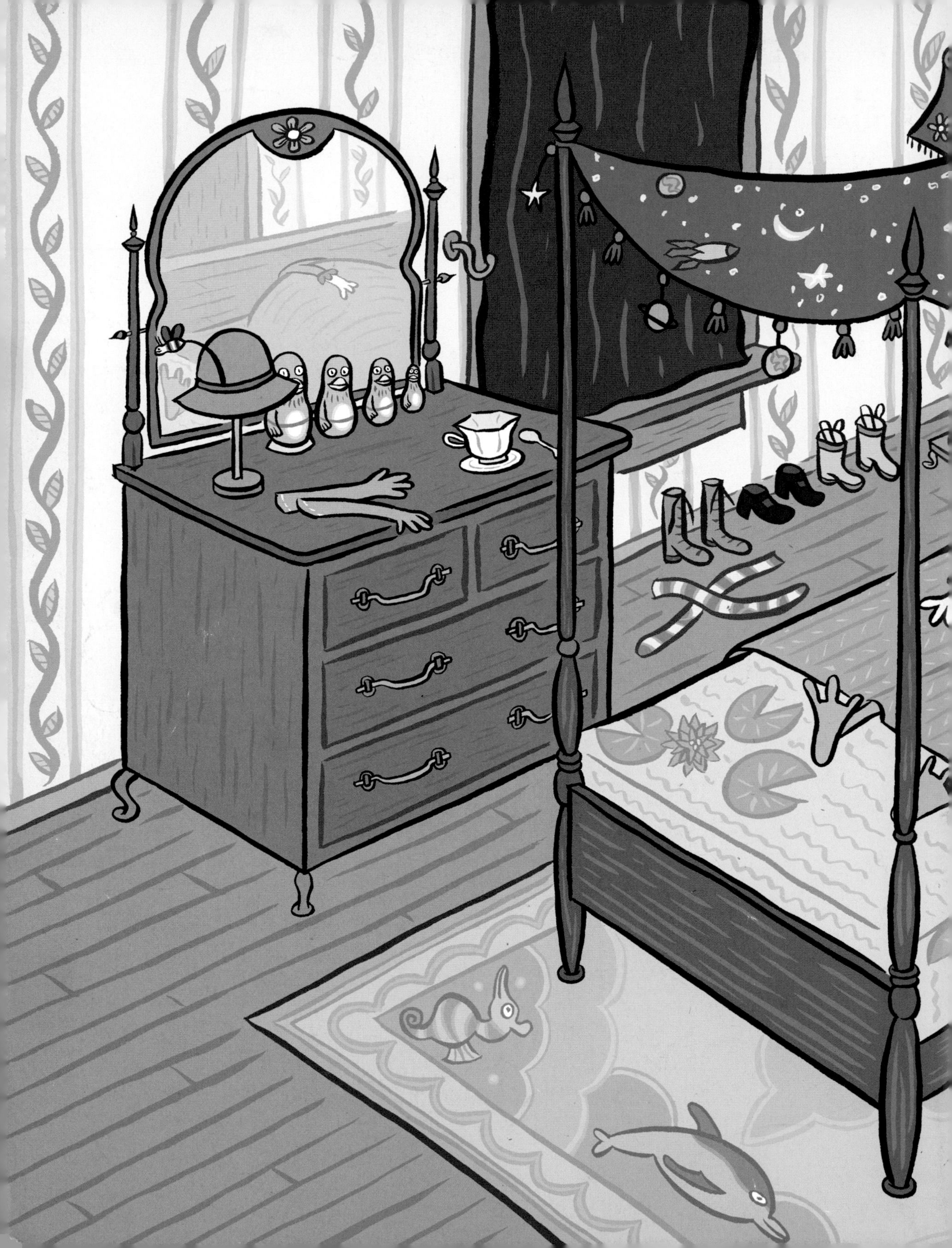

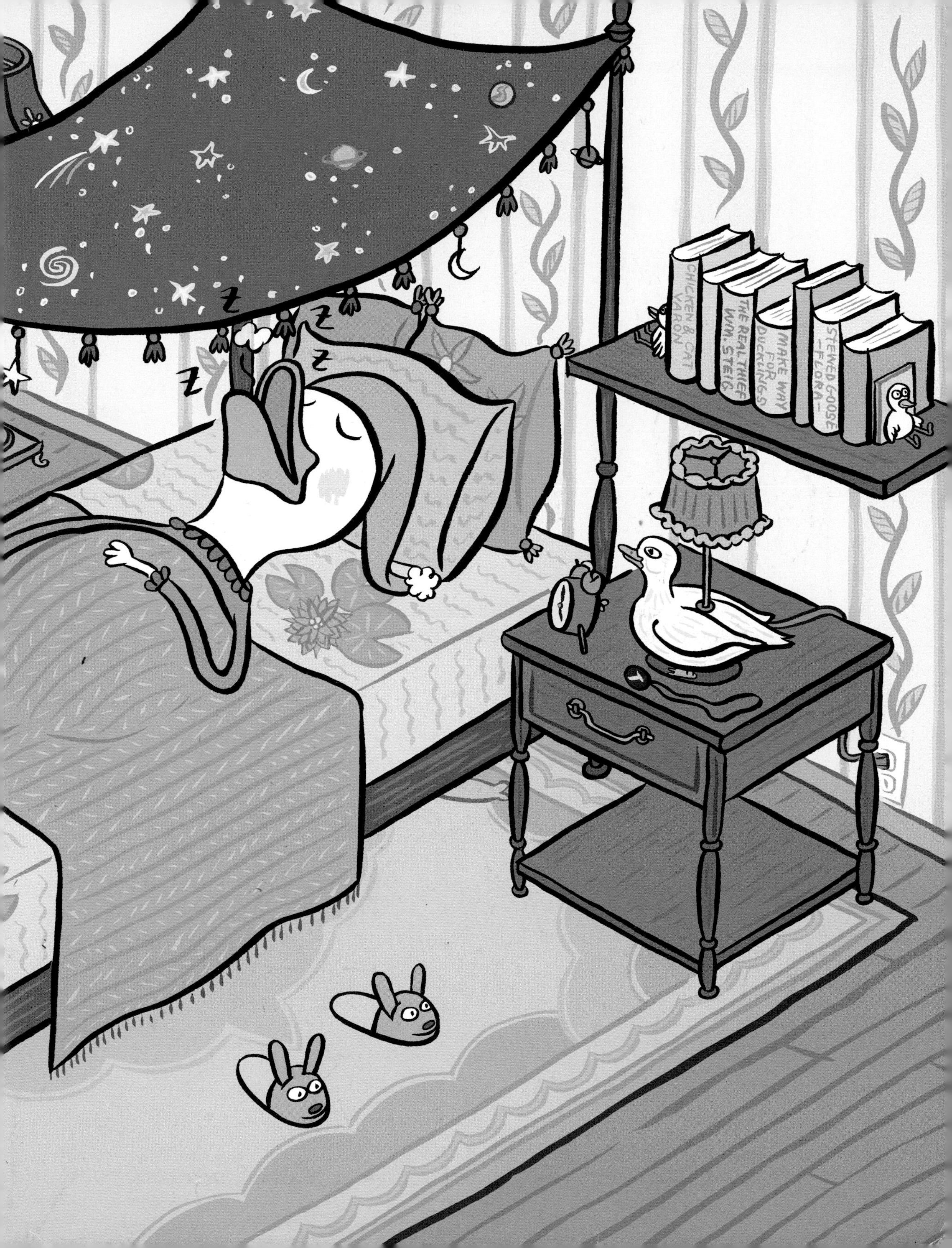
Z
Z
Z
Z
CHICKEN & CAT VARON
THE REAL THIEF WM. STEIG
MAKE WAY FOR DUCKLINGS
STEWED GOOSE —FLORA—

CHAPTER

theodora's days were very busy.

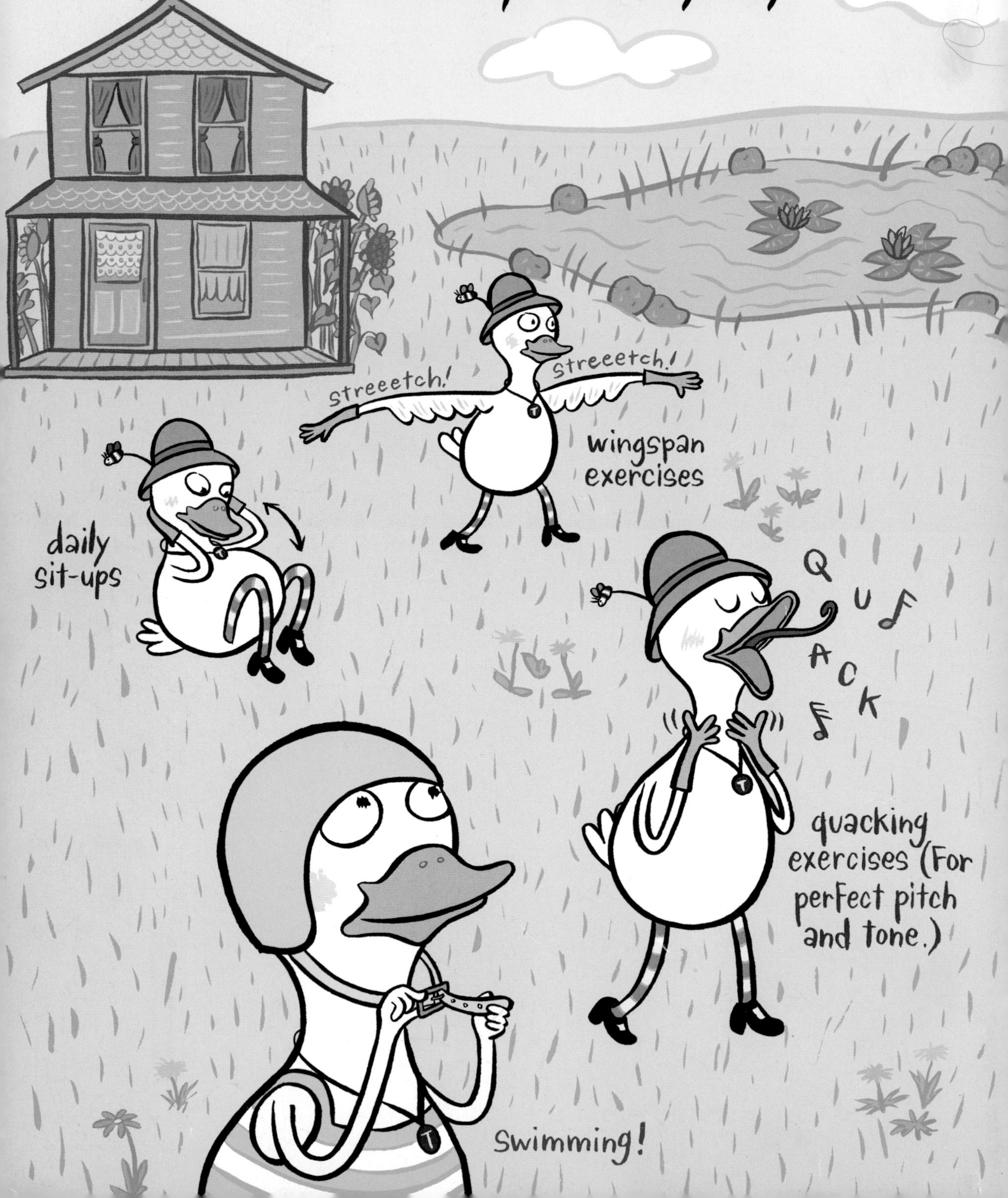
streeetch!
streeetch!
wingspan exercises
daily sit-ups
Q U A C K
quacking exercises (For perfect pitch and tone.)
Swimming!

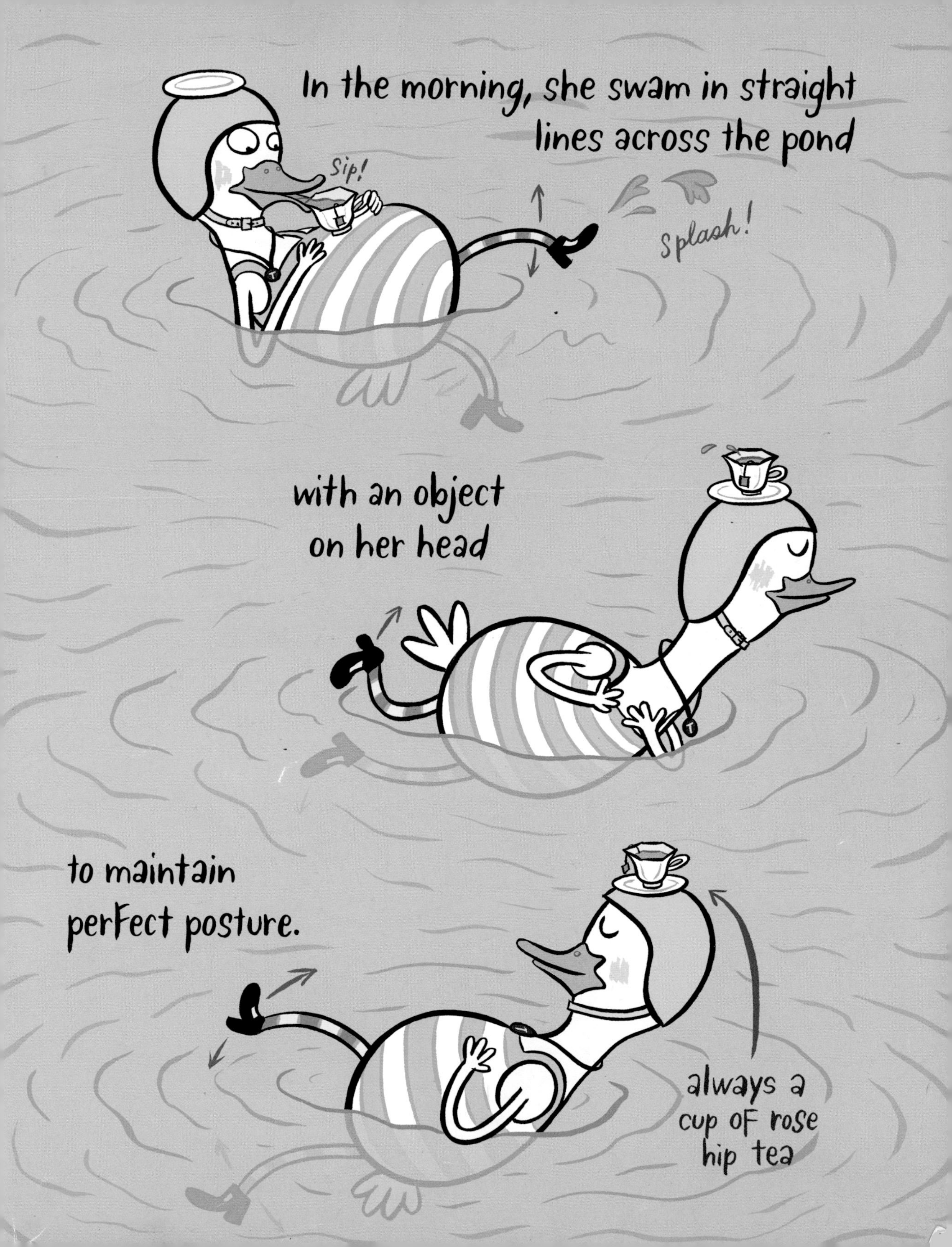
In the morning, she swam in straight lines across the pond
Sip!
Splash!
with an object on her head
to maintain perfect posture.
always a cup of rose hip tea

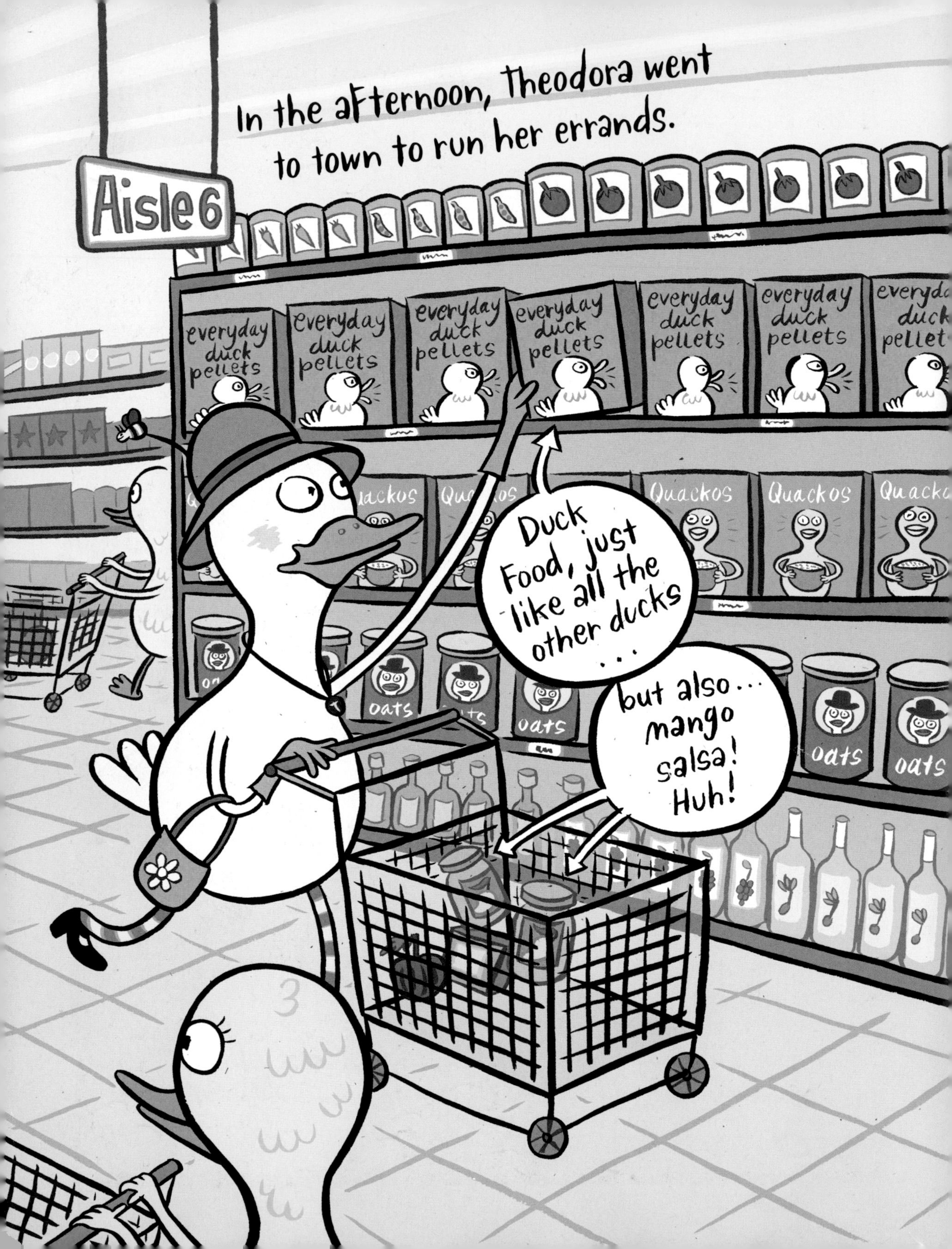
In the afternoon, Theodora went to town to run her errands.
Aisle 6
everyday duck pellets
Quackos
oats
Duck Food, just like all the other ducks . . .
but also... mango salsa! Huh!

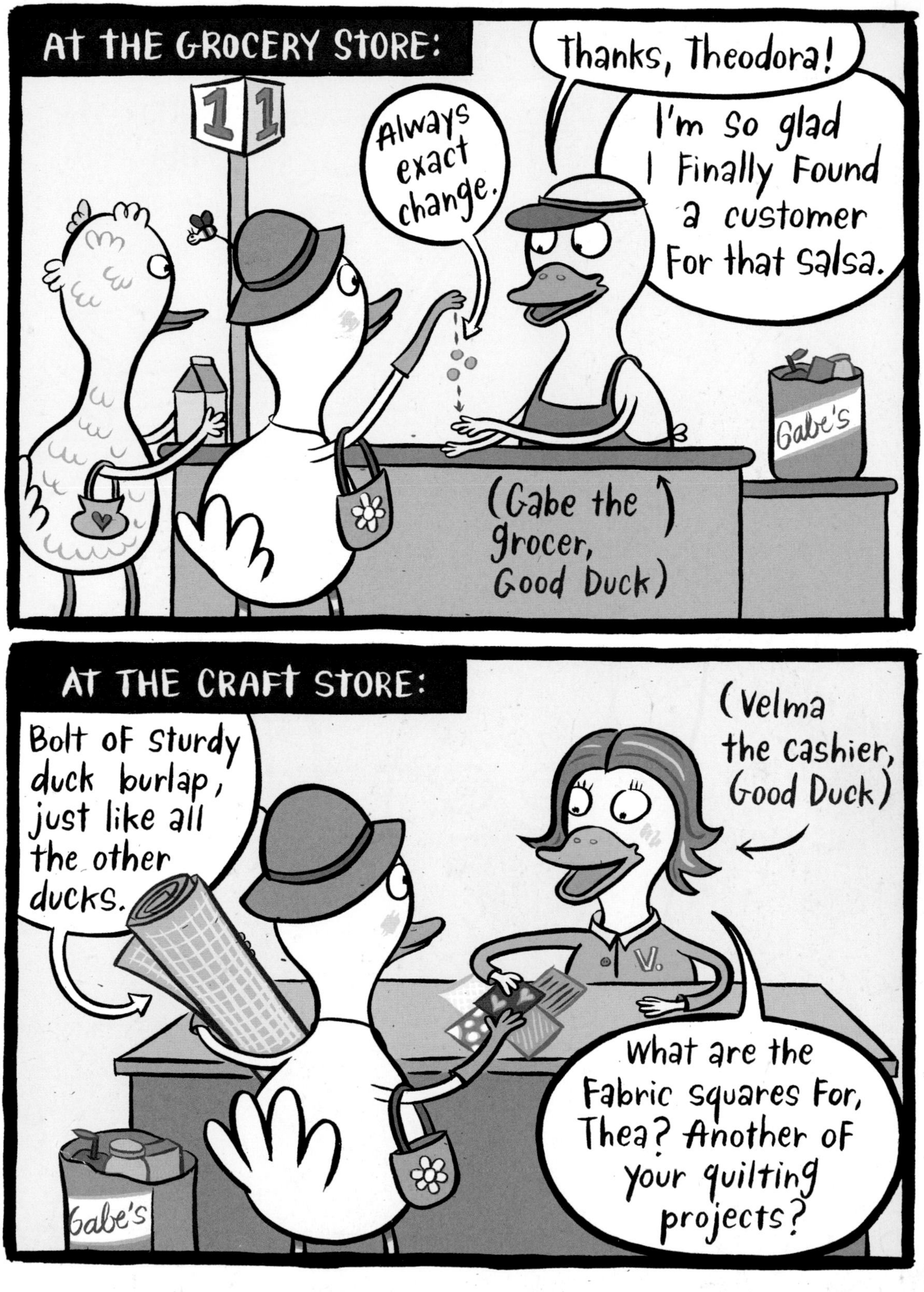
AT THE GROCERY STORE:
11
Always exact change.
Thanks, Theodora!
I'm so glad I finally found a customer for that salsa.
(Gabe the grocer, Good Duck)
Gabe's
AT THE CRAFT STORE:
Bolt of sturdy duck burlap, just like all the other ducks.
(Velma the cashier, Good Duck)
V.
What are the fabric squares for, Thea? Another of your quilting projects?
Gabe's

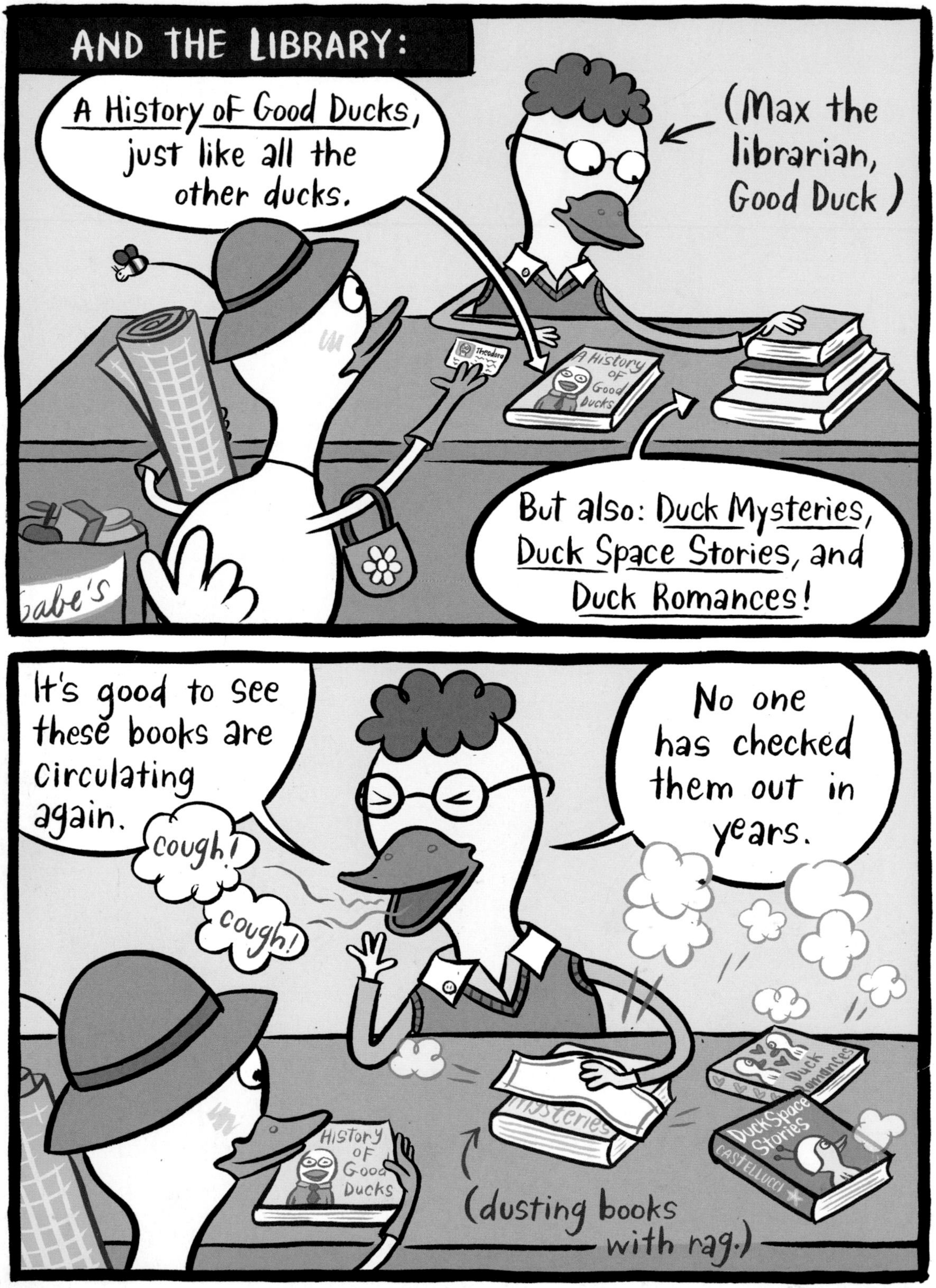
AND THE LIBRARY:
A History of Good Ducks, just like all the other ducks.
(Max the librarian, Good Duck)
Theodore
A History of Good Ducks
Gabe's
But also: Duck Mysteries, Duck Space Stories, and Duck Romances!
It's good to see these books are circulating again.
cough!
cough!
No one has checked them out in years.
History of Good Ducks
Mysteries
Duck Romances
Duck Space Stories
CASTELLUCCI
(dusting books with rag.)

Then Theodora would pedal home.
She never flew, even though her wings
were in tip-top shape.

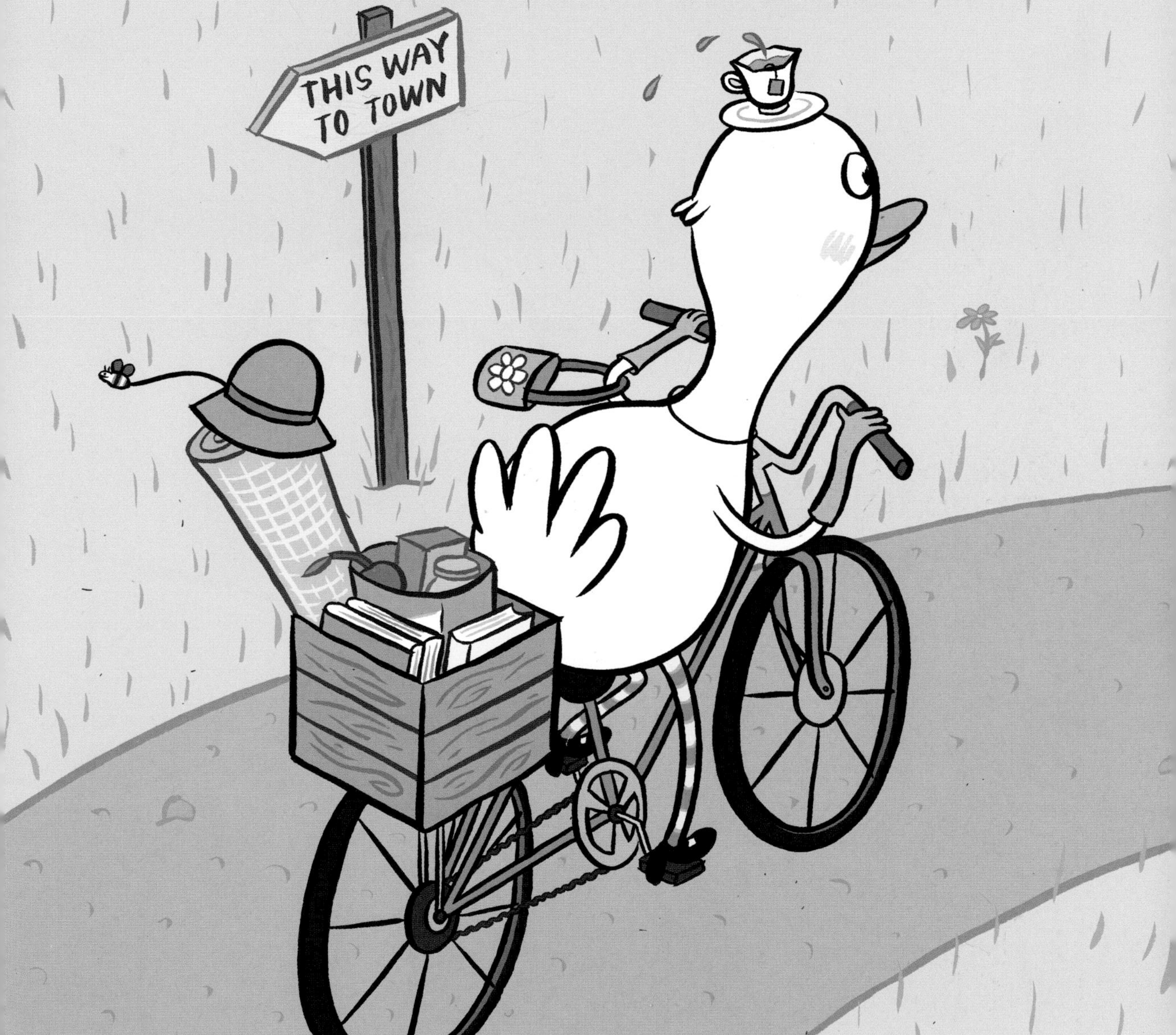
THIS WAY
TO TOWN

She enjoyed living close to town, but not
too close. Theodora Duck liked to be alone.

Every night Theodora fixed herself a fine supper, gazed up at the stars, and made a wish on the first star she saw.

(knows all her constellations, of course)

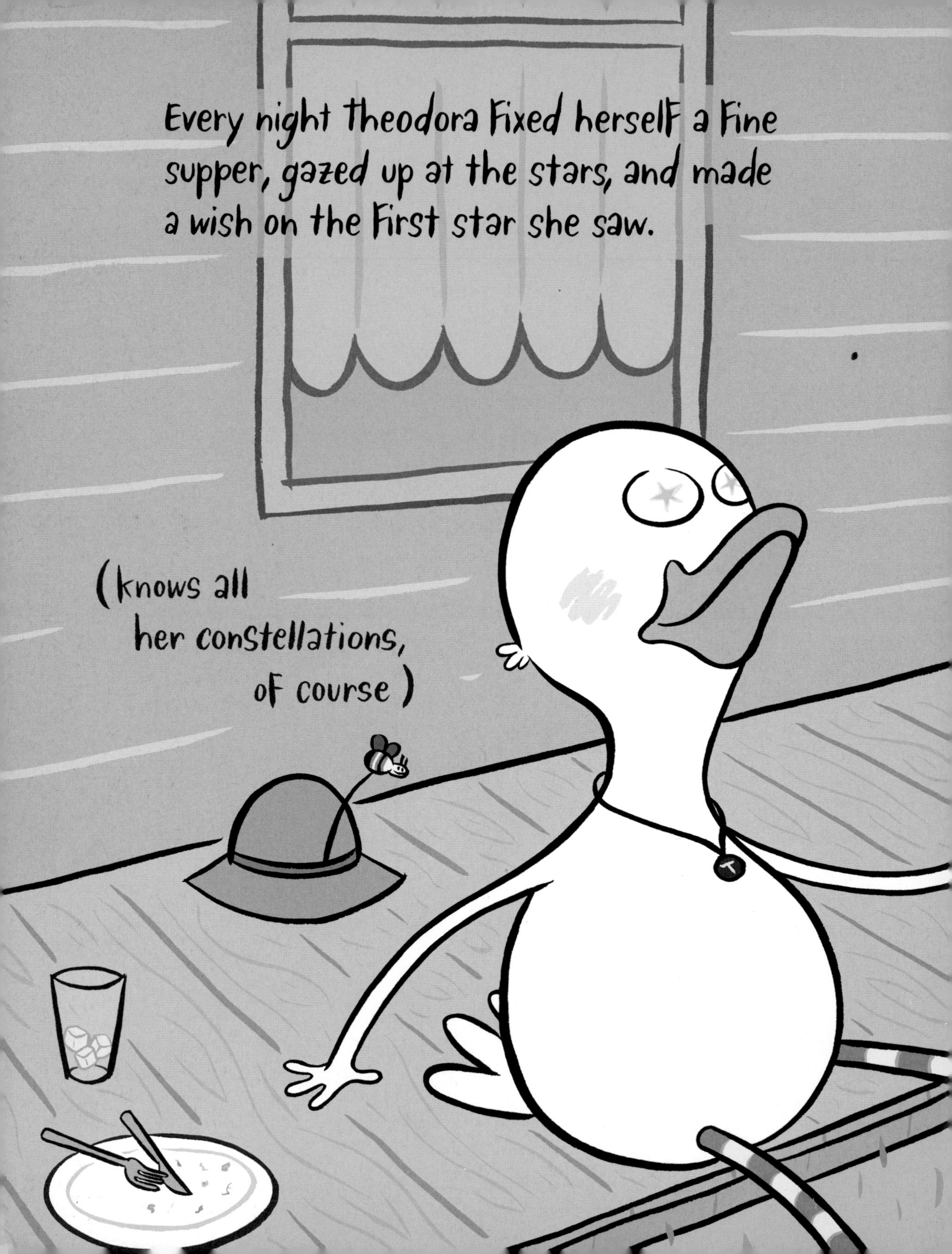

(Ursa Minor)

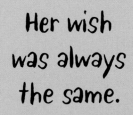

Her wish
was always
the same.

theodora wished that nothing in her happy life would ever change.

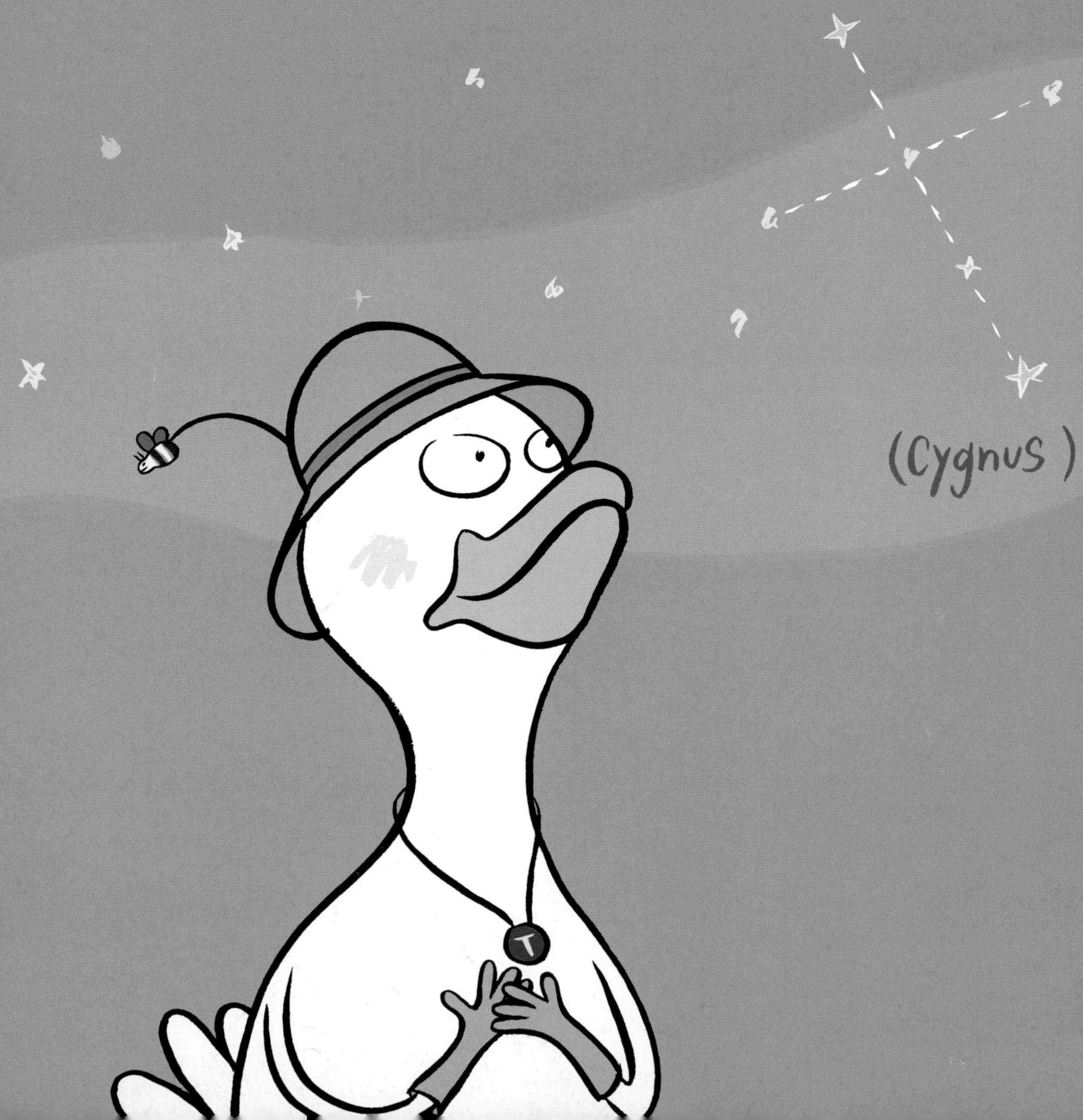
(Cygnus)

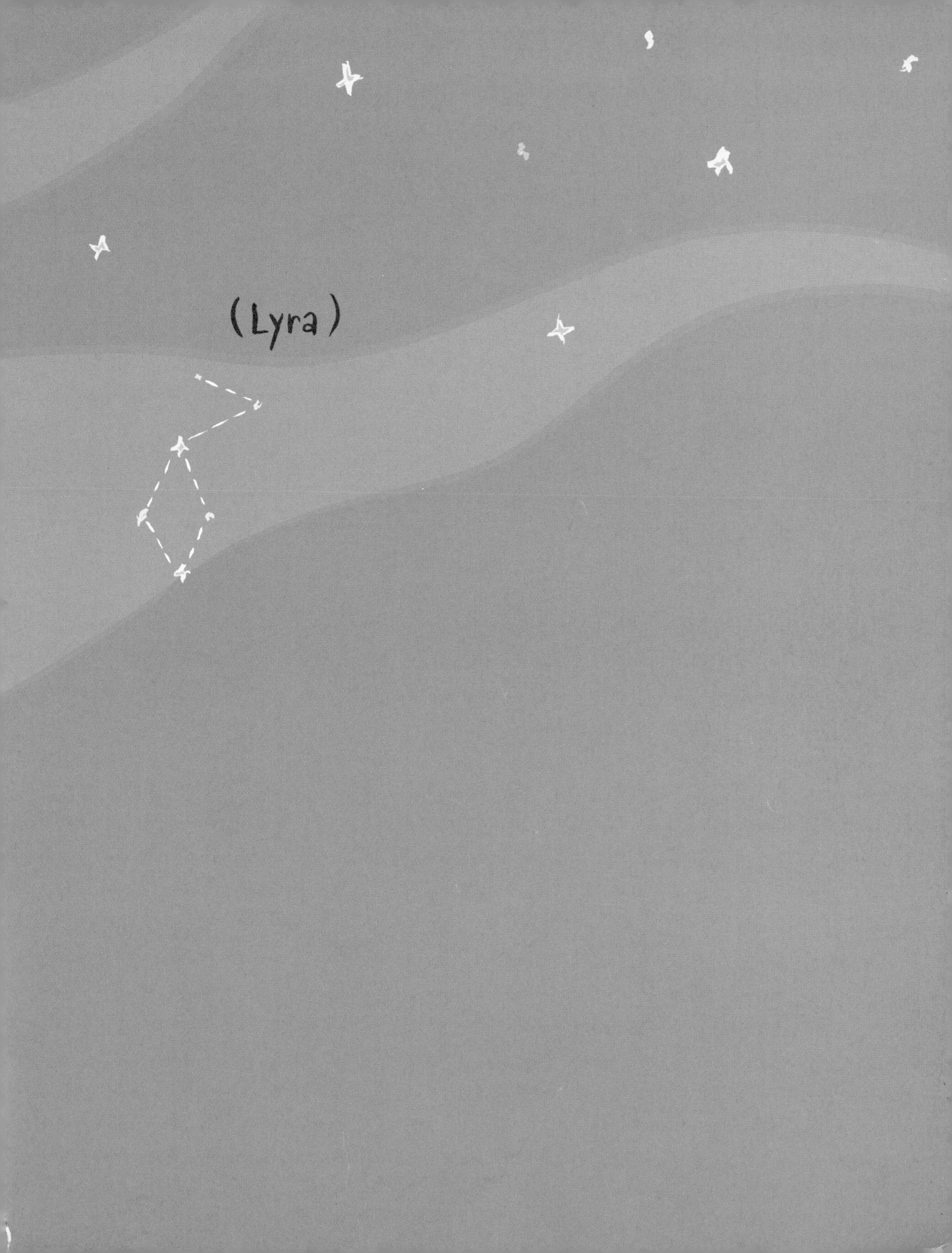
(Lyra)

CHAPTER

One day, Theodora noticed something strange.

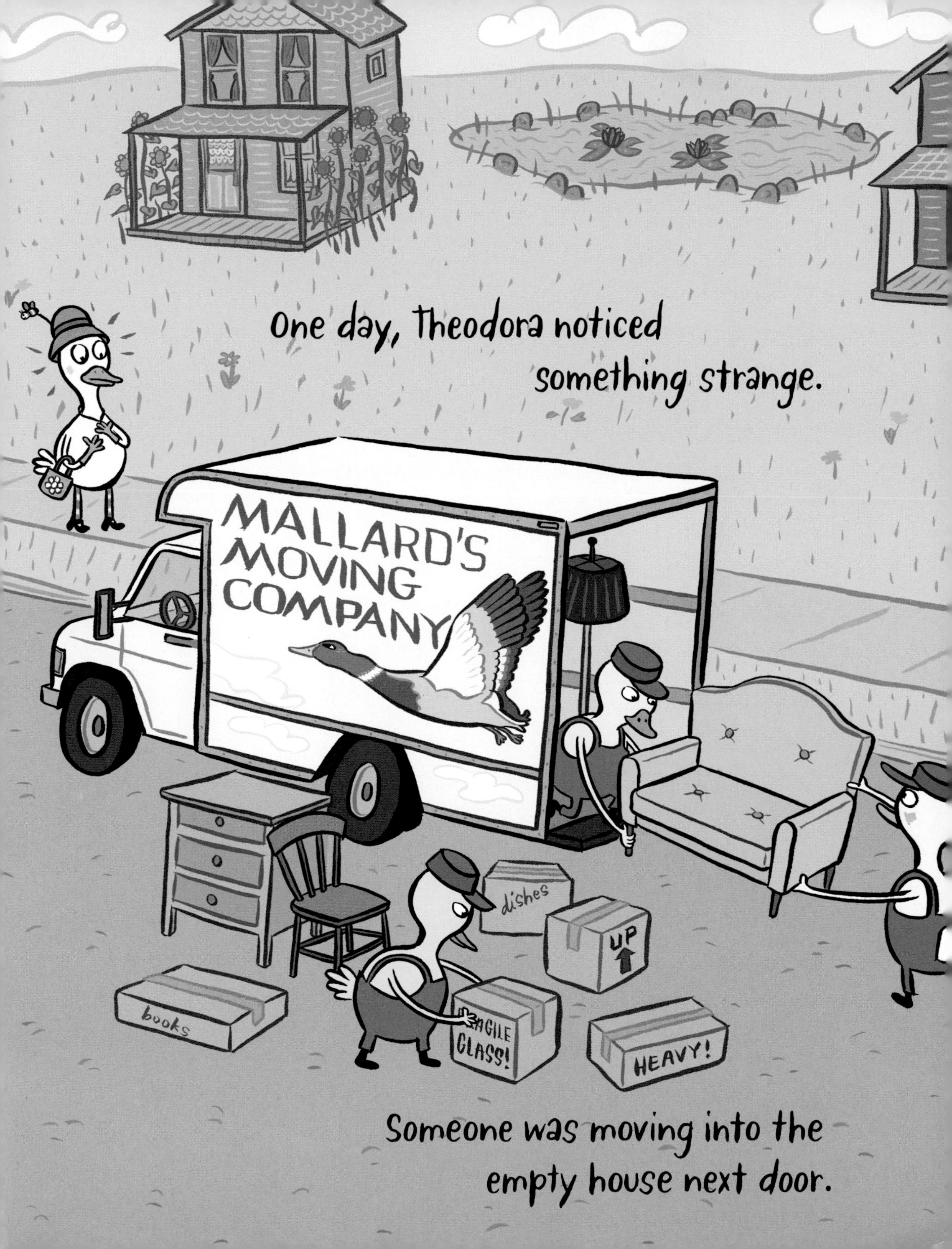
MALLARD'S MOVING COMPANY
dishes
UP
books
GLASS!
HEAVY!

Someone was moving into the empty house next door.

the new neighbor had set up all kinds of gadgets and sculptures that were both modern and strange.

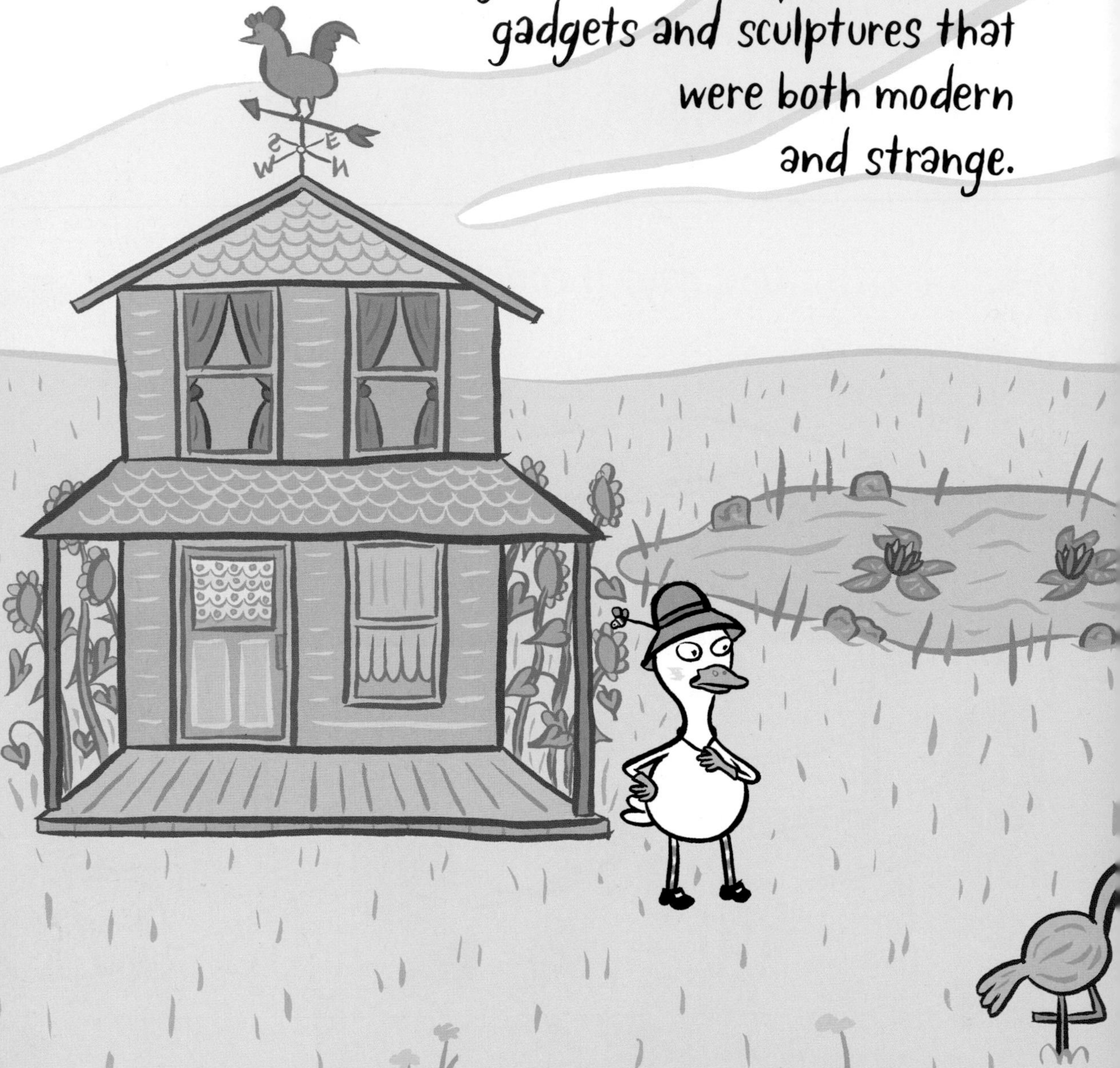

After a few days, it was clear the new duck intended to stay.

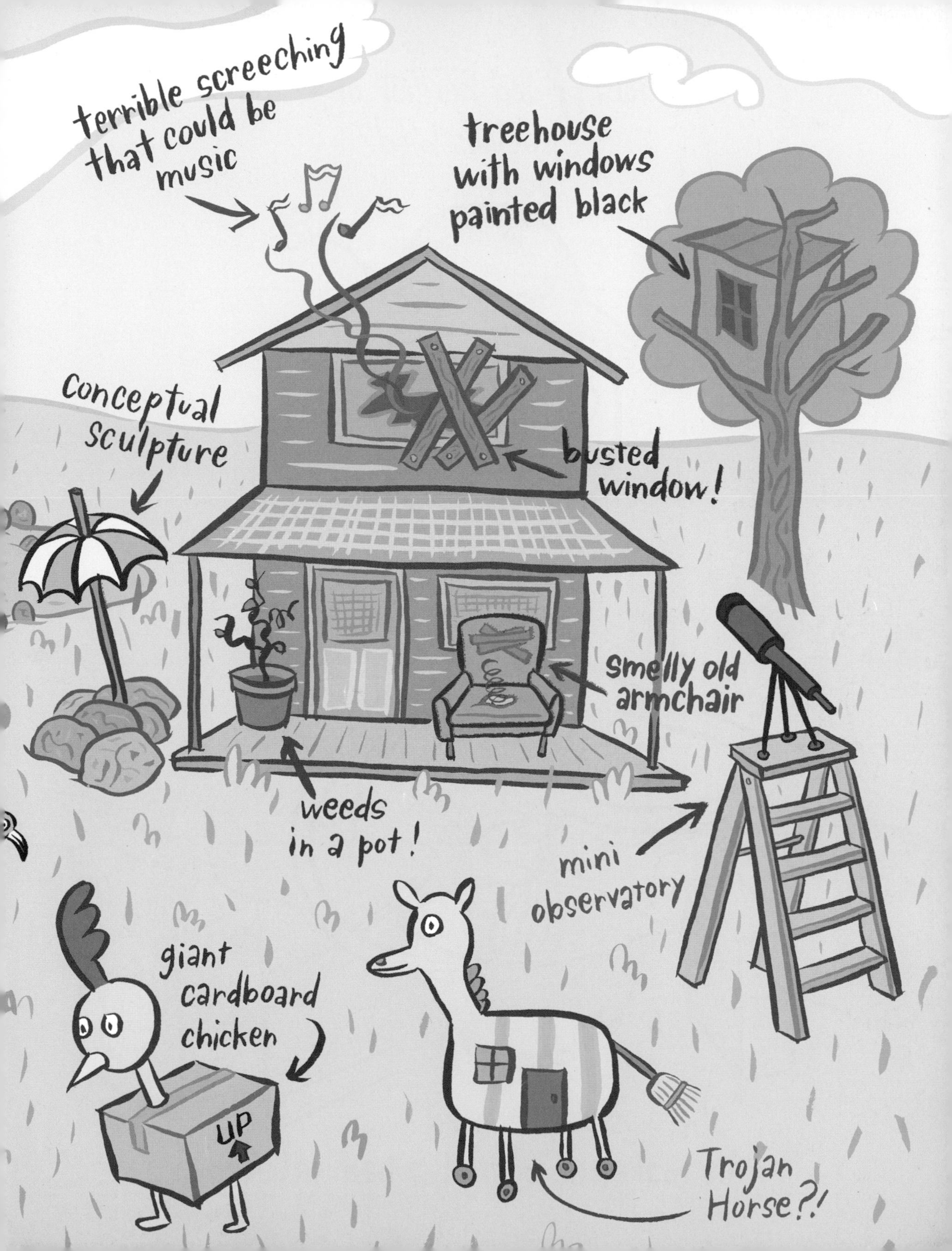
terrible screeching that could be music
treehouse with windows painted black
conceptual sculpture
busted window!
smelly old armchair
weeds in a pot!
mini observatory
giant cardboard chicken
UP
Trojan Horse?!

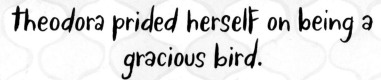

theodora prided herself on being a gracious bird.

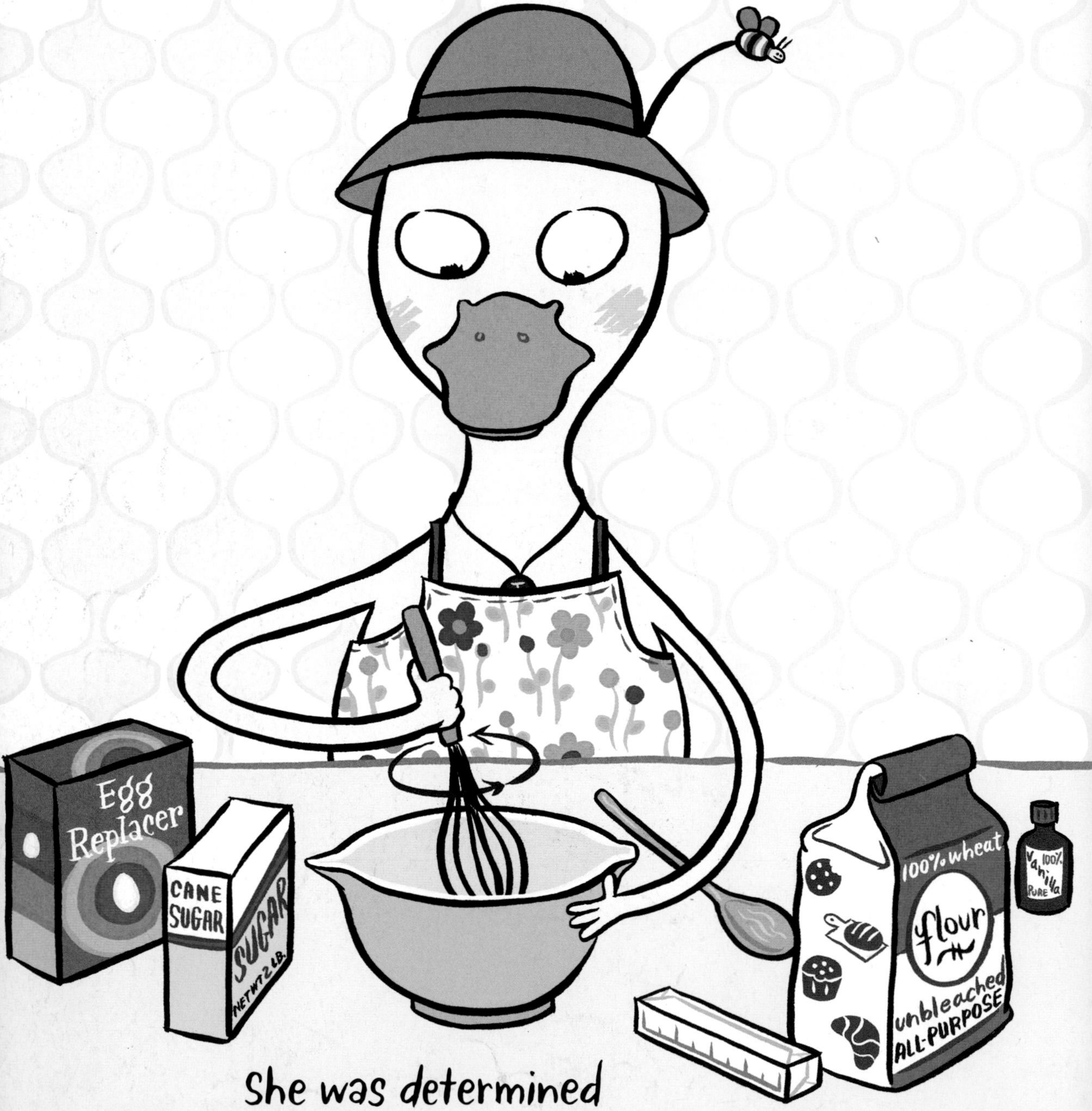
Egg Replacer
CANE SUGAR
SUGAR
NET WT 2 LB.
100% wheat
flour
unbleached ALL-PURPOSE
100% Vanilla PURE

She was determined to make the best of a bad situation.

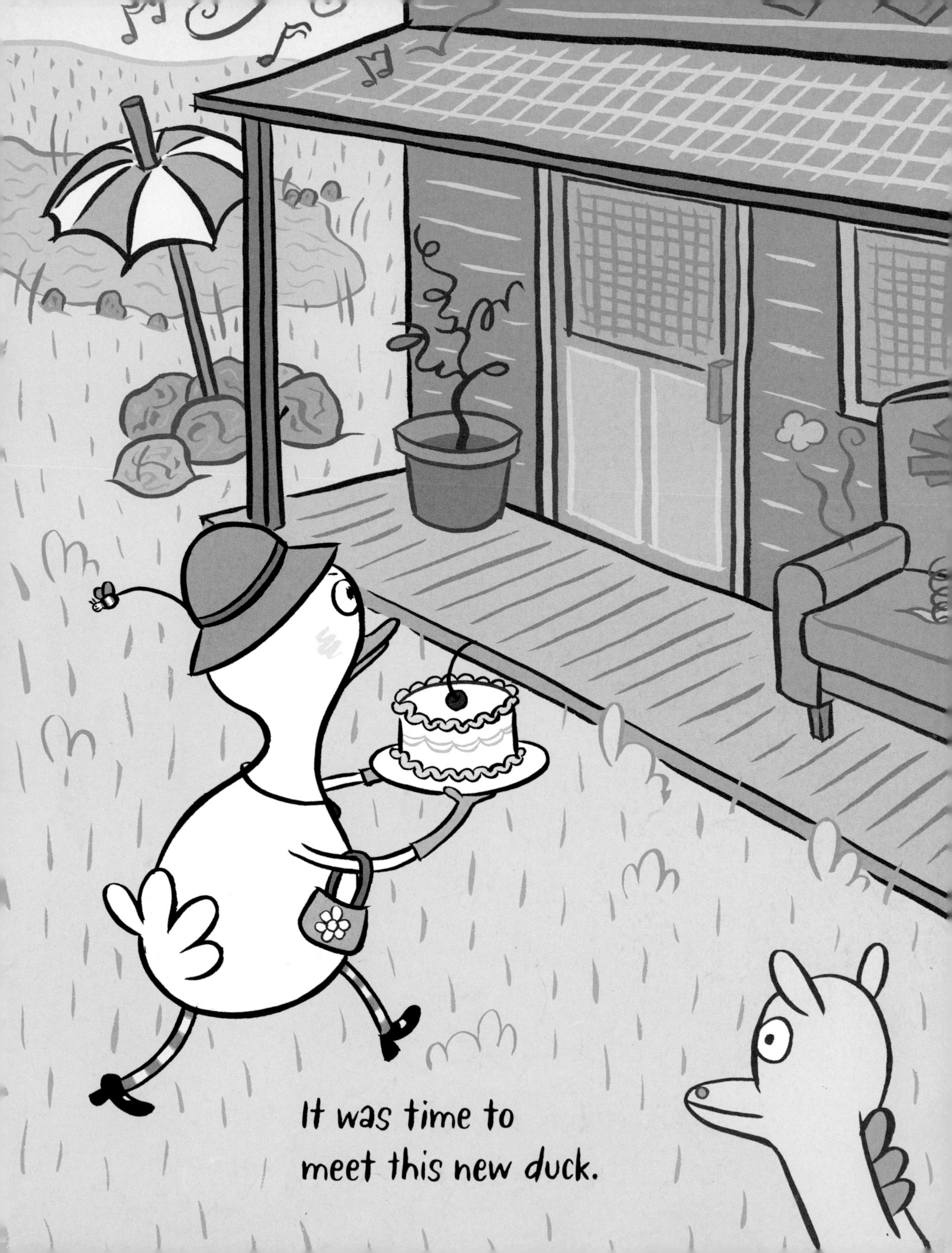

It was time to
meet this new duck.

She Found him sunbathing in the backyard. Theodora looked the new duck over.

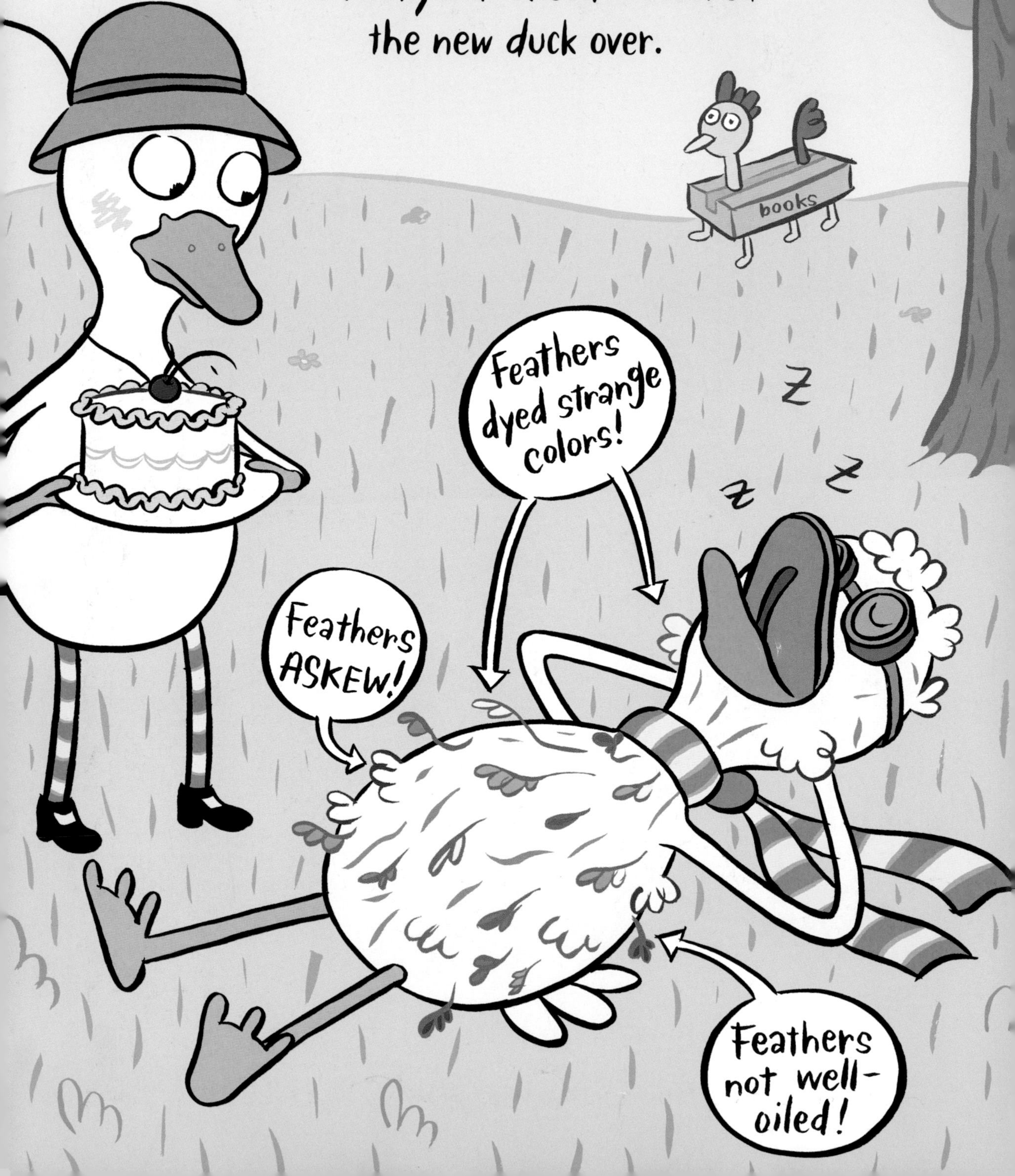
books
Feathers dyed strange colors!
Feathers ASKEW!
Feathers not well-oiled!

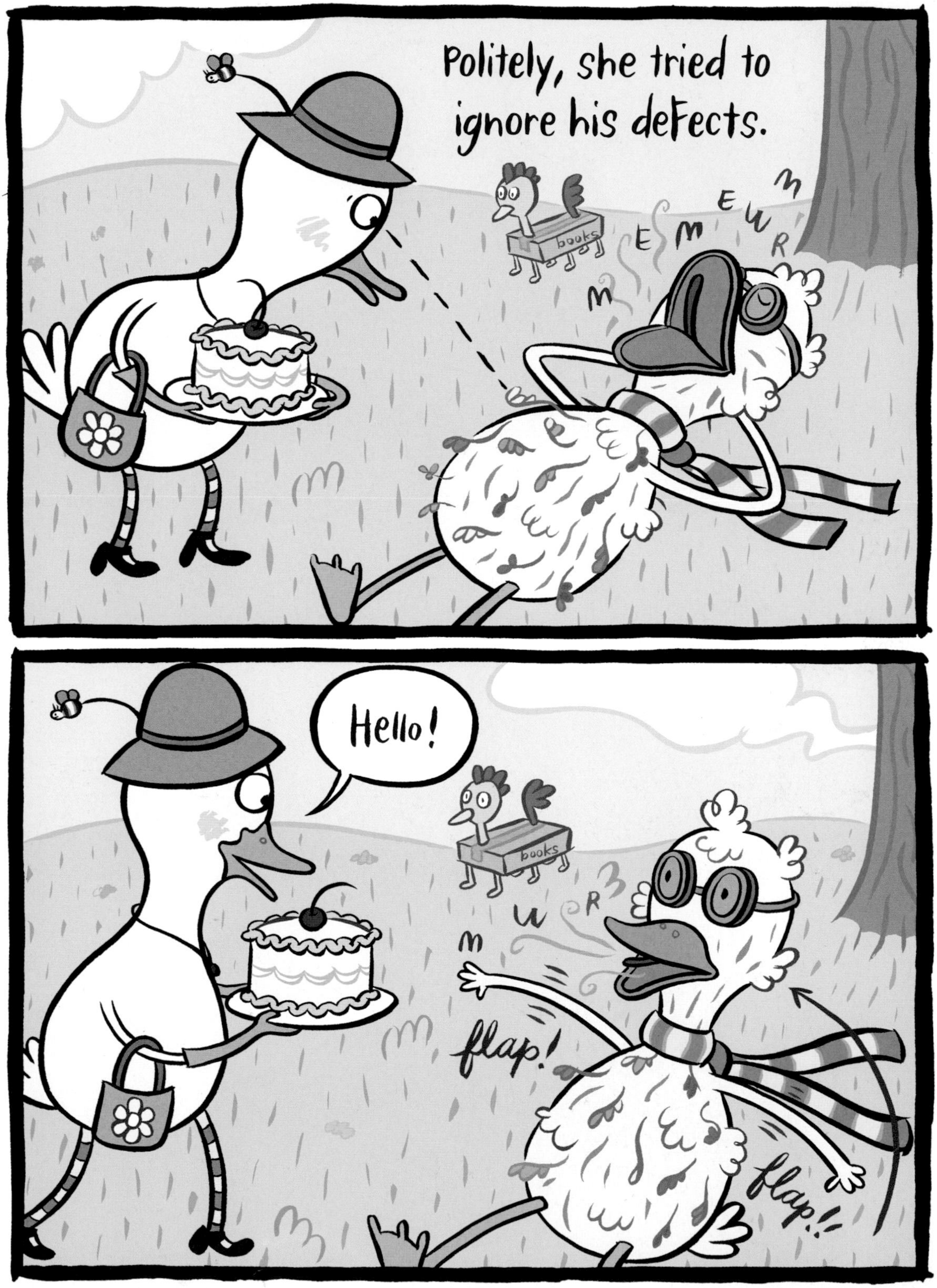
Politely, she tried to ignore his defects.
books
Hello!
books
flap!
flap!!

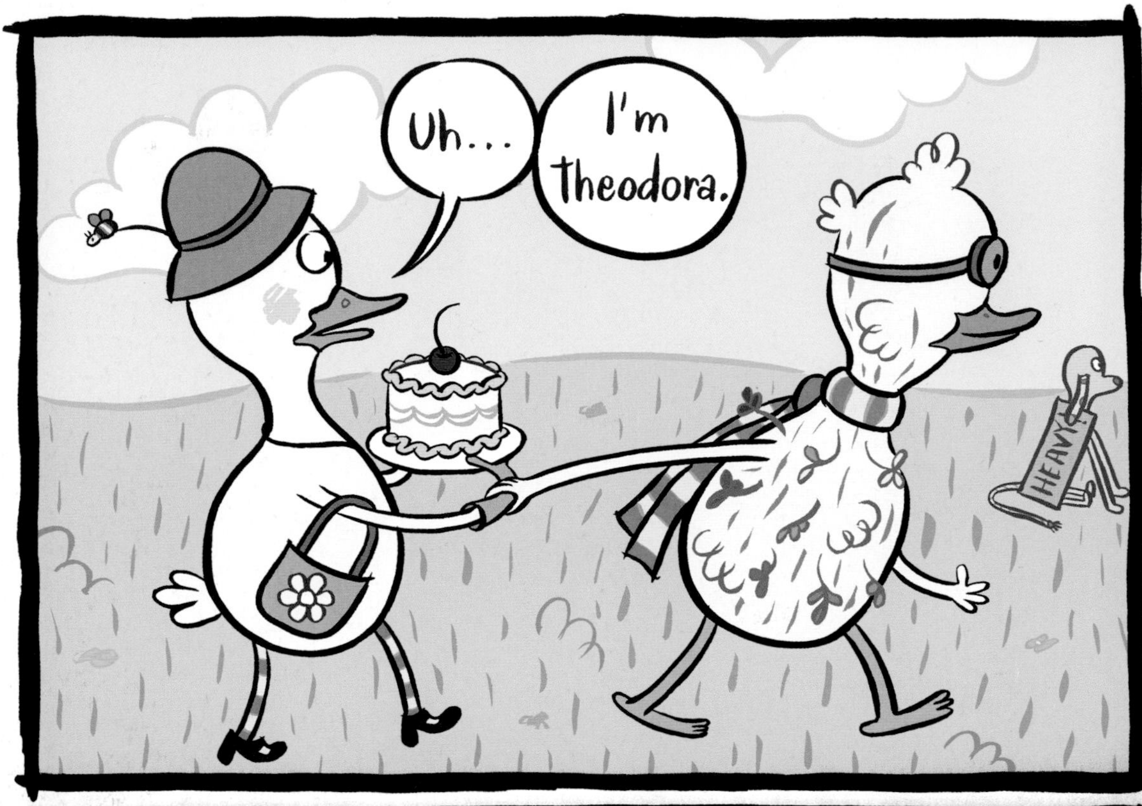
Uh...
I'm theodora.
HEAVY

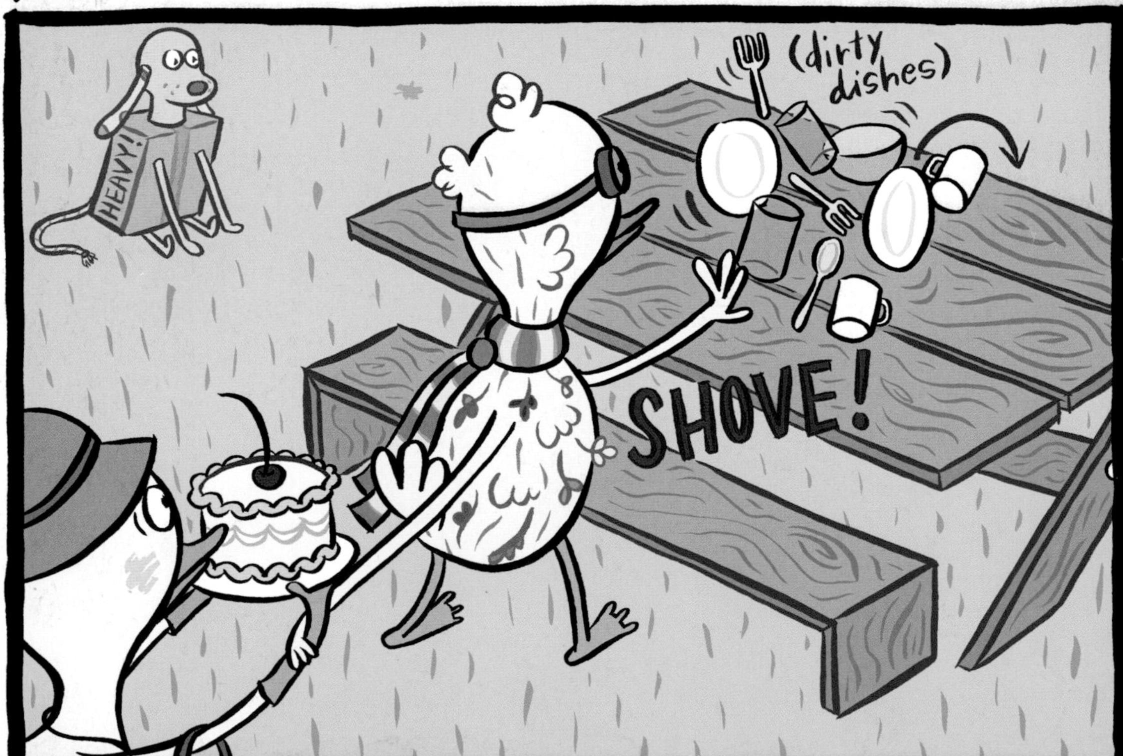
HEAVY!
(dirty dishes)
SHOVE!

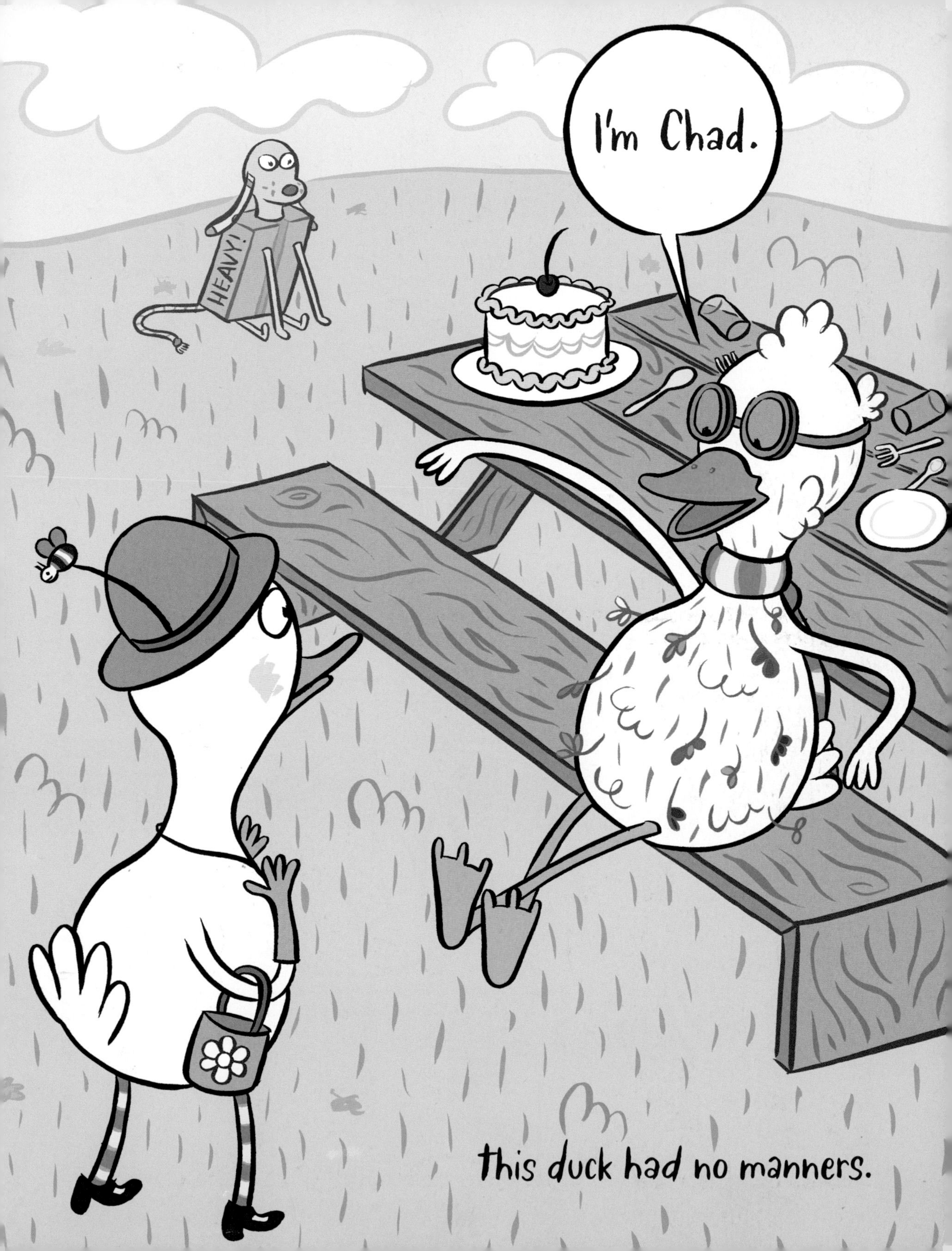
HEAVY!
I'm Chad.
this duck had no manners.

theodora daintily sliced him a piece of cake anyway because that's what good ducks do.

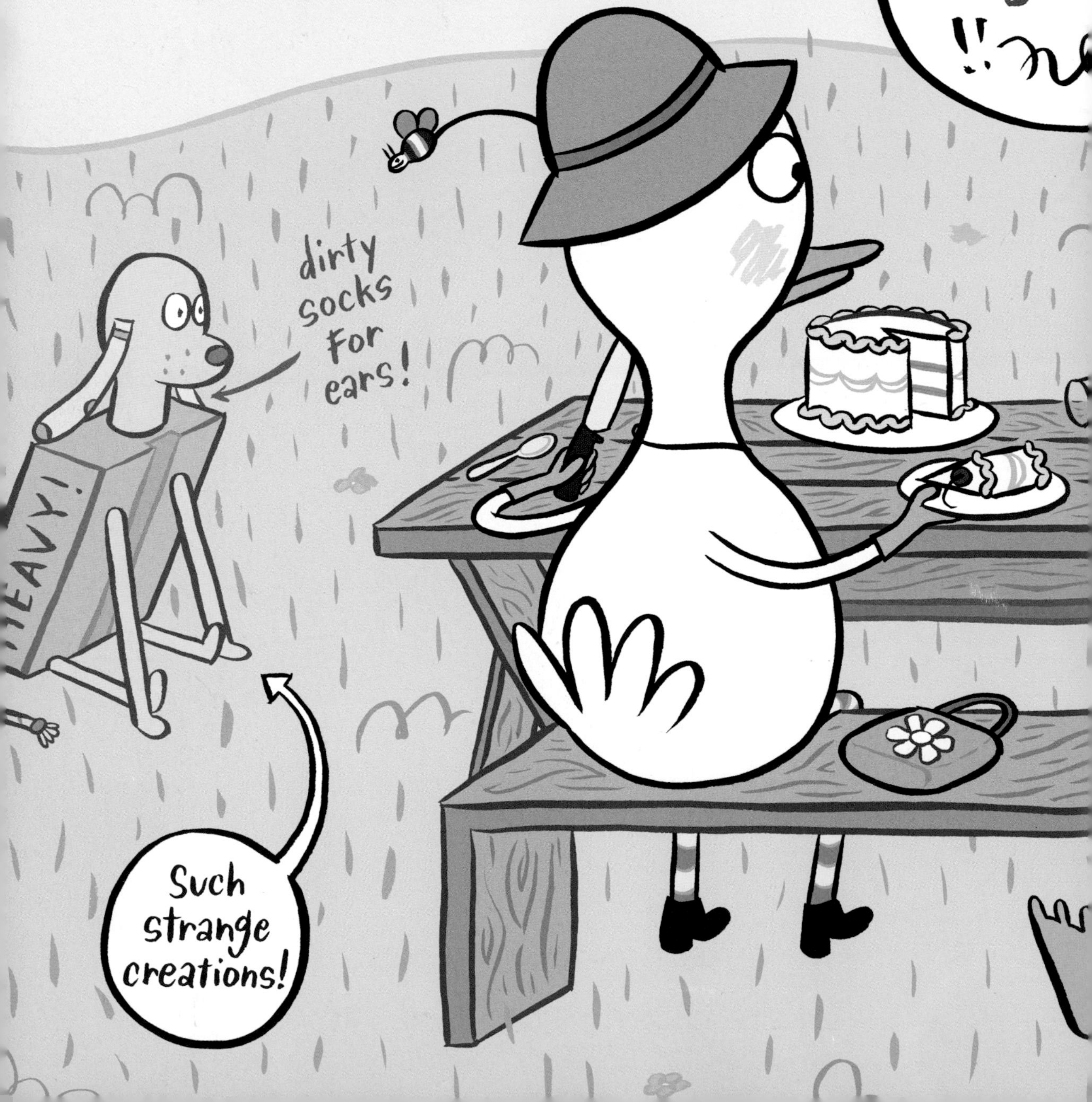

dirty socks for ears!
HEAVY!
Such strange creations!

And then Chad began to talk:

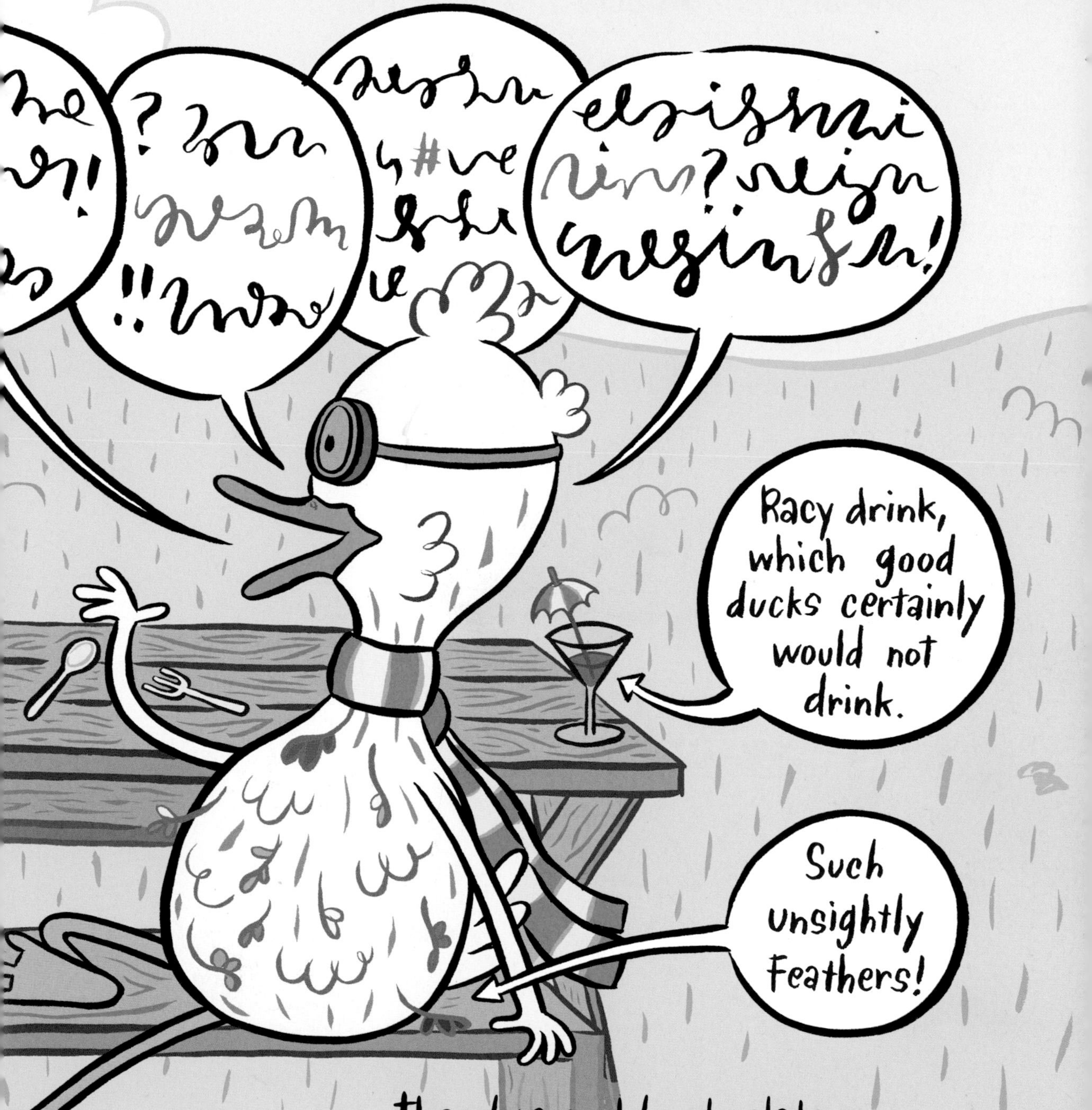

Racy drink, which good ducks certainly would not drink.
Such unsightly Feathers!

Theodora could not relate
to a single thing that he said.
But she knew one thing was certain . . .

She and Chad would <u>not</u> be friends.

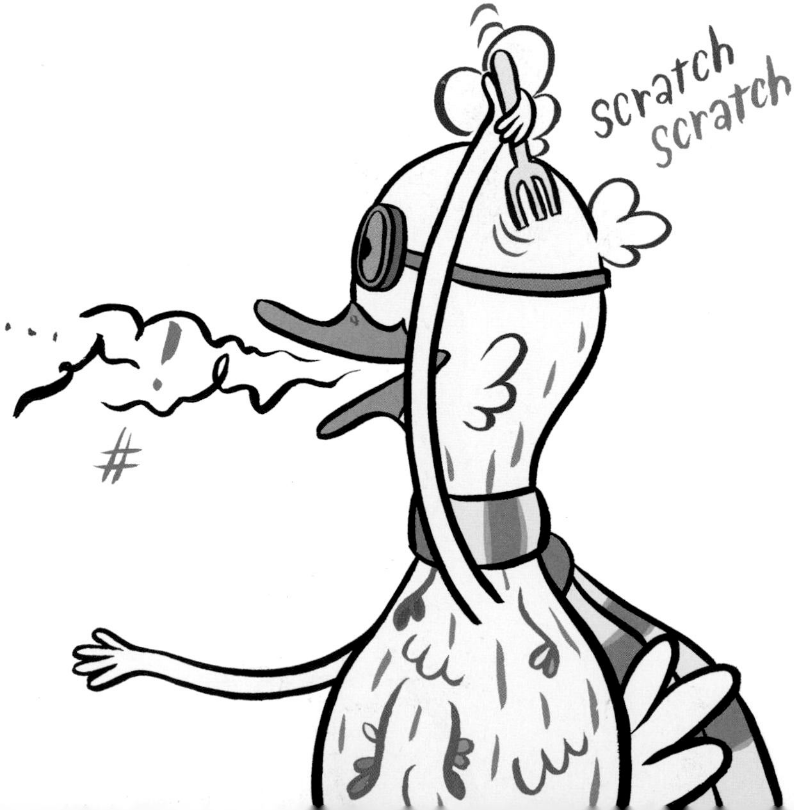
scratch
scratch

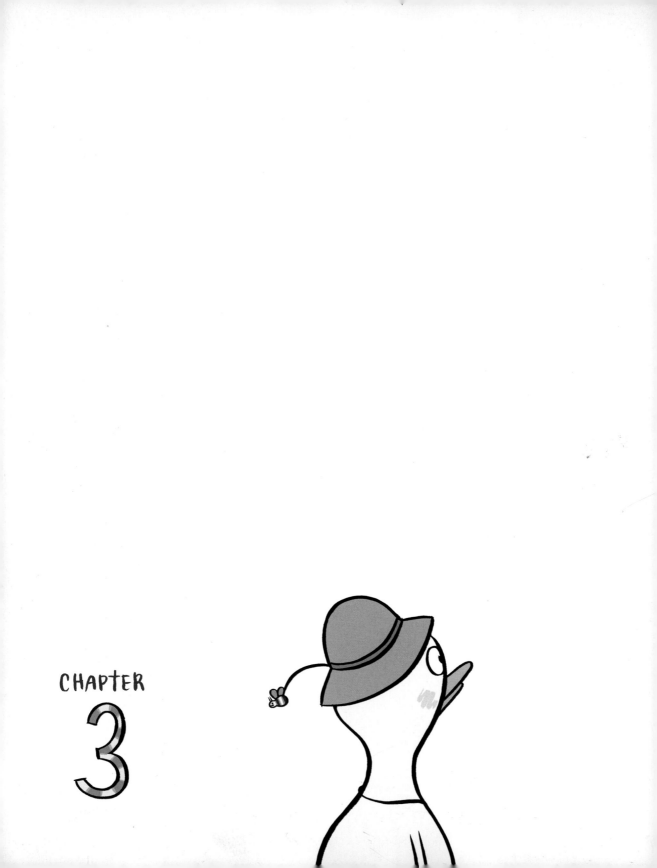

CHAPTER

3

theodora decided to keep to herself.

Chad was not her style of duck.

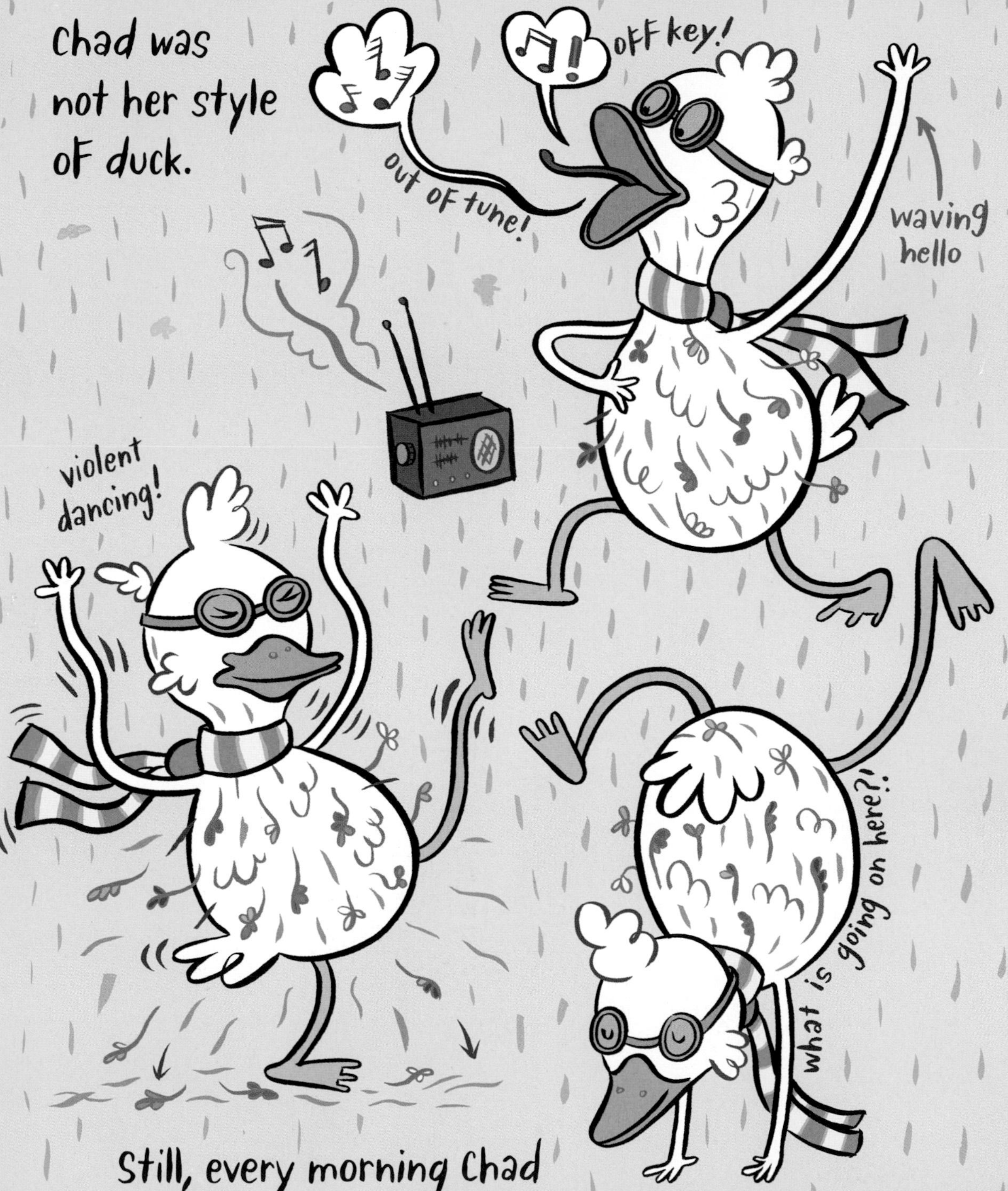
off key!
out of tune!
waving hello
violent dancing!
what is going on here?!

Still, every morning Chad would wave to Theodora as he did his exercises.

then there was his swimming!!

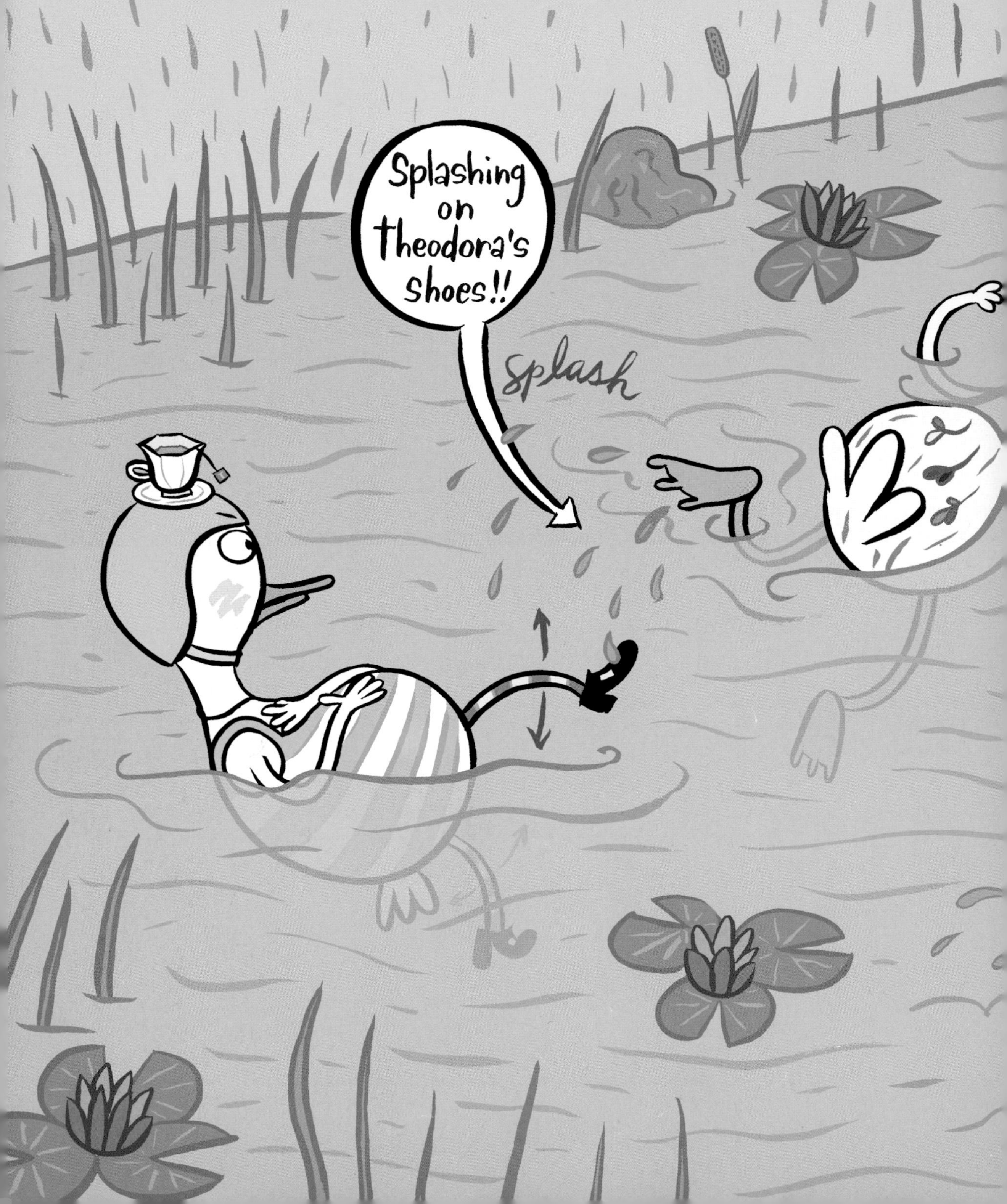
Splashing on theodora's shoes!!
splash

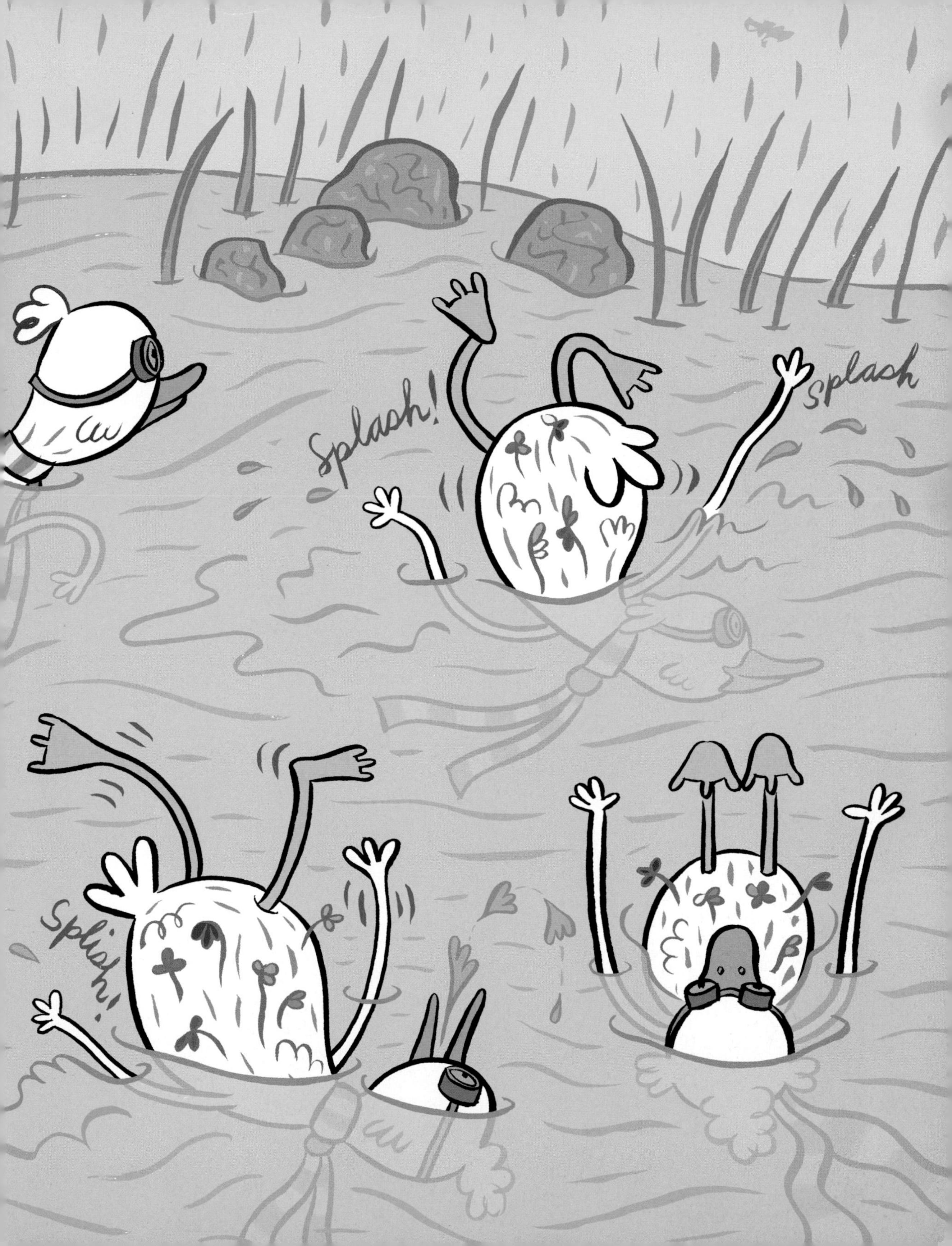
Splash!
Splash
Splish!

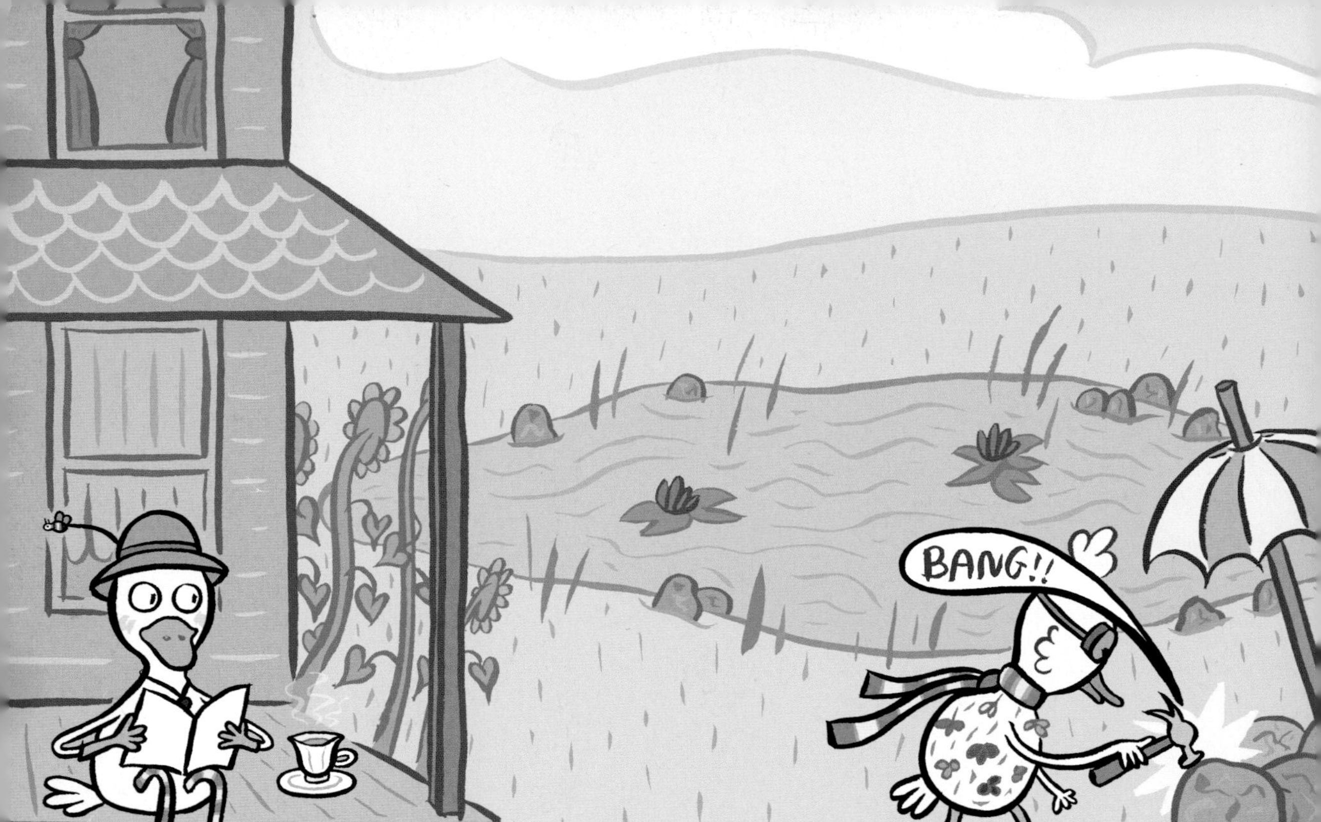
BANG!!

And in the afternoons,
Chad would spend hours hammering away
at the large objects that he called art
and proudly displayed in his yard.

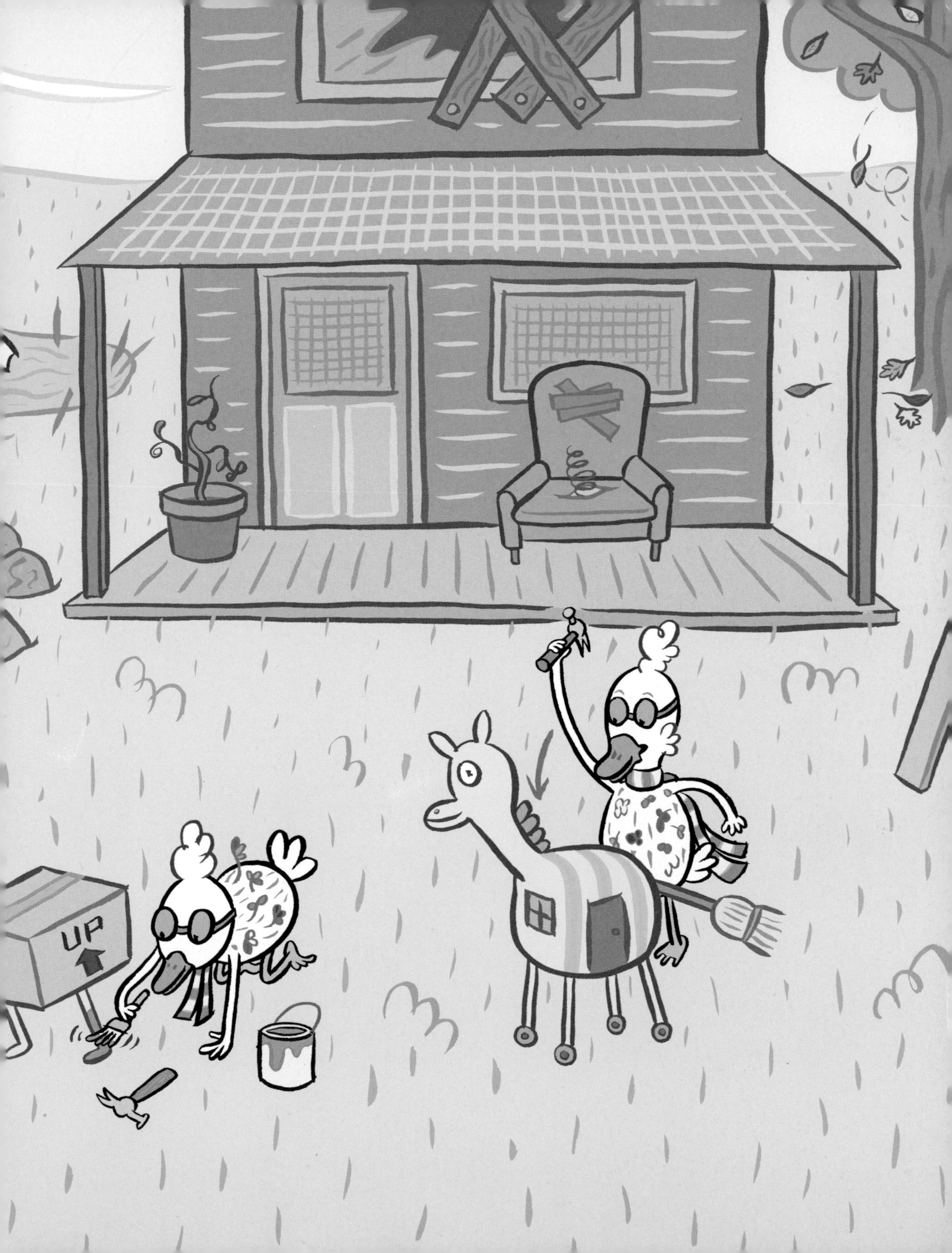
UP

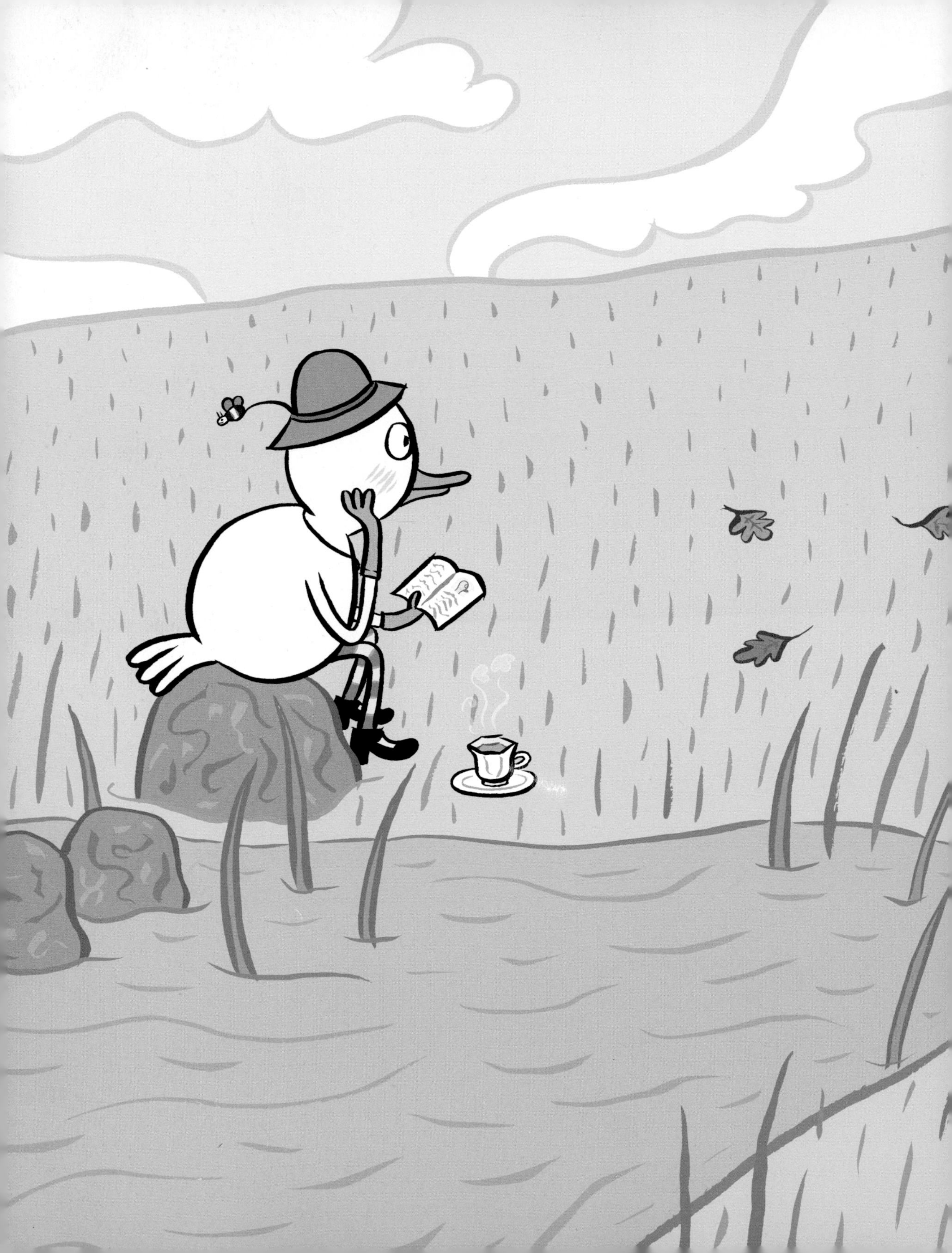

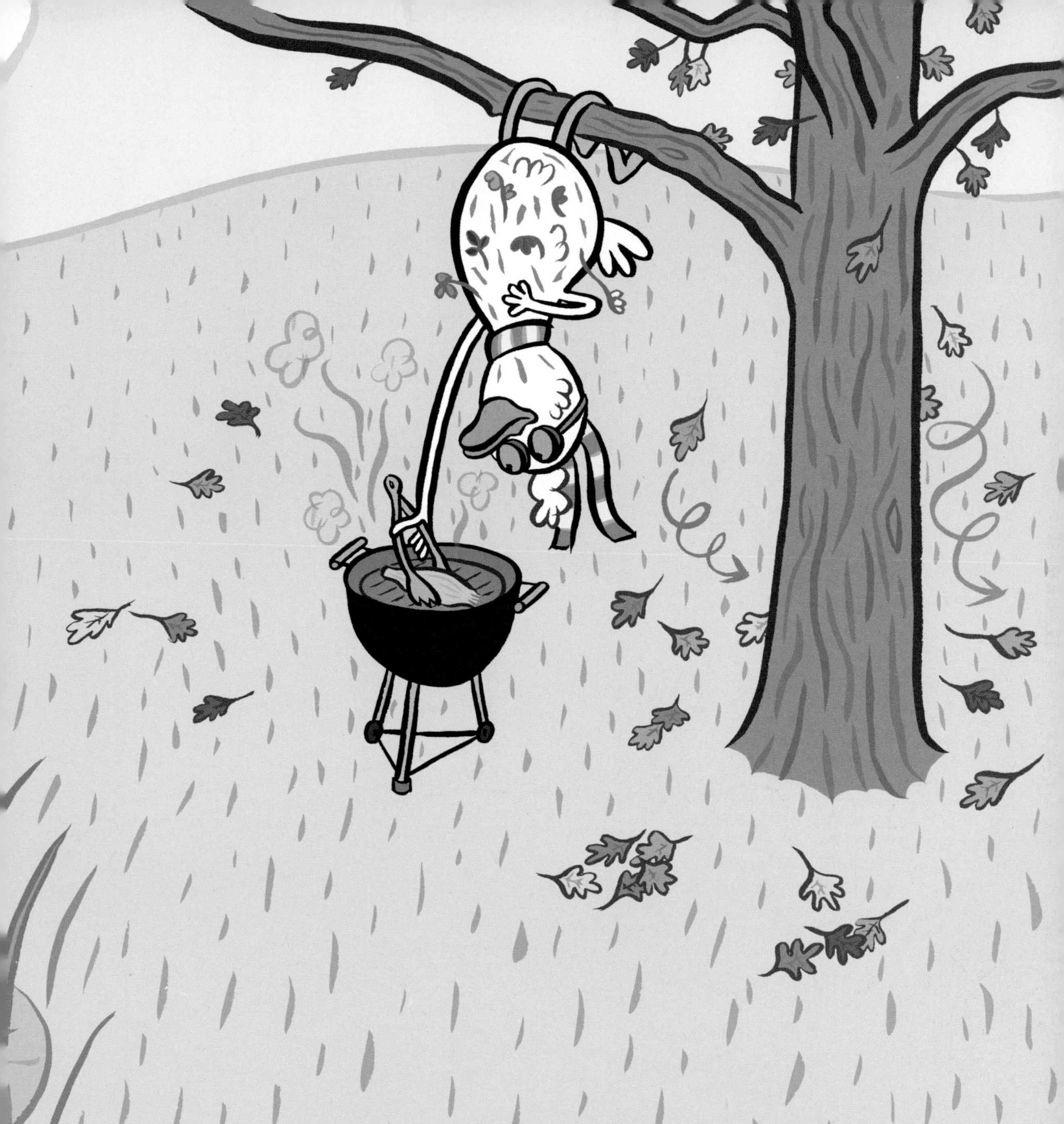

"Well," thought Theodora,
"It's nearly winter. Chad will go
south soon enough."

theodora always meant to Fly south For winter. But she never did, preFerring instead the calm quiet oF the pond in winter.

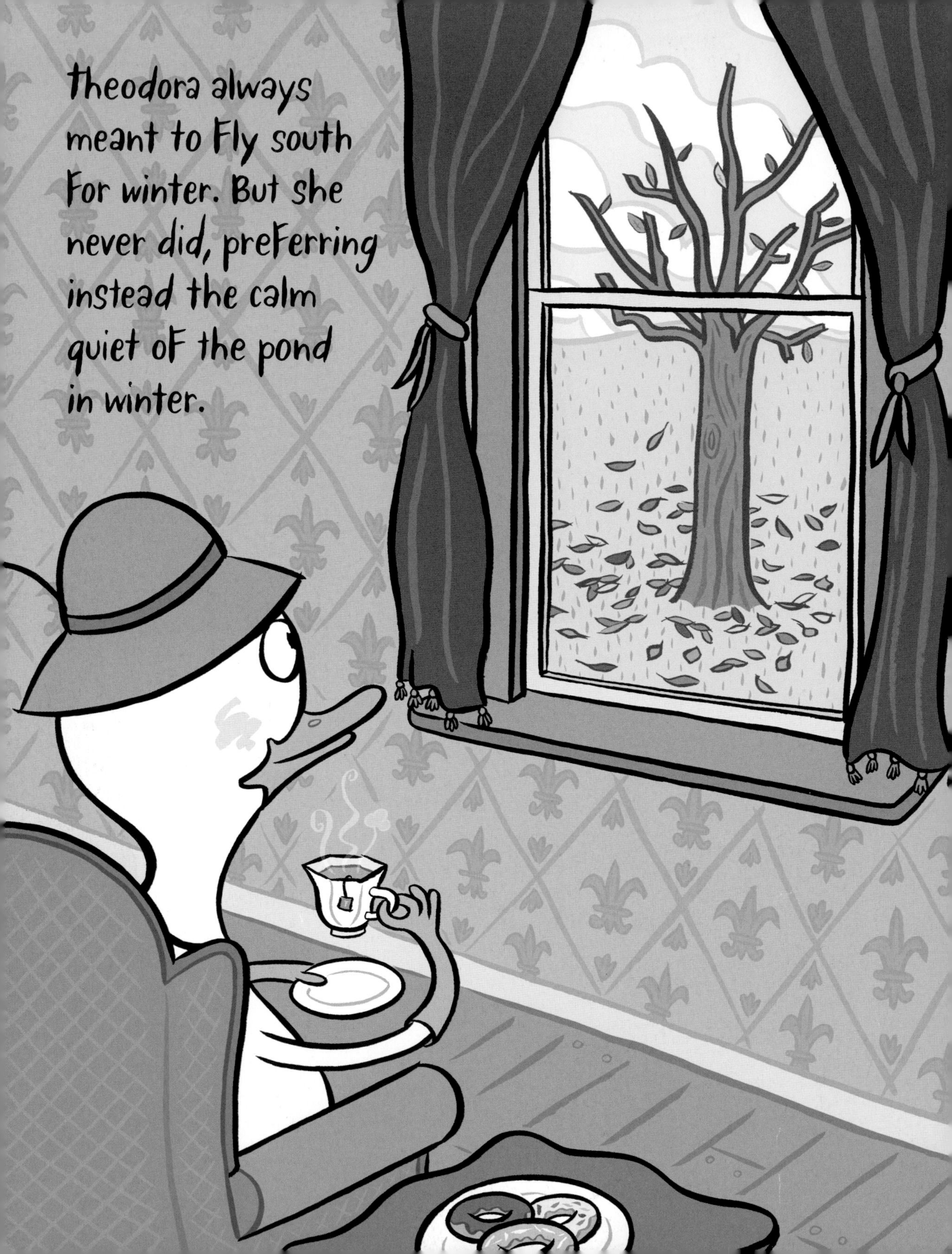

All the same, Theodora liked to watch
the other ducks Fly south.

From the ground,
they looked so mighty and beautiful.

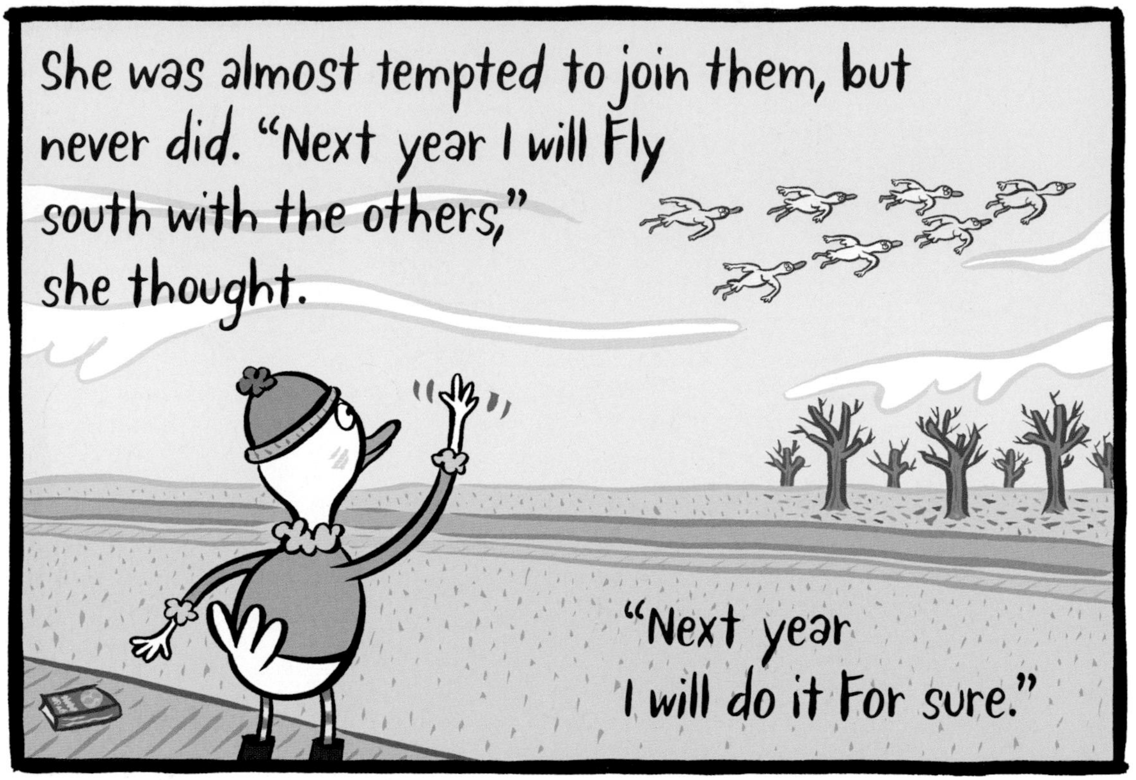
She was almost tempted to join them, but never did. "Next year I will fly south with the others," she thought.
"Next year I will do it for sure."

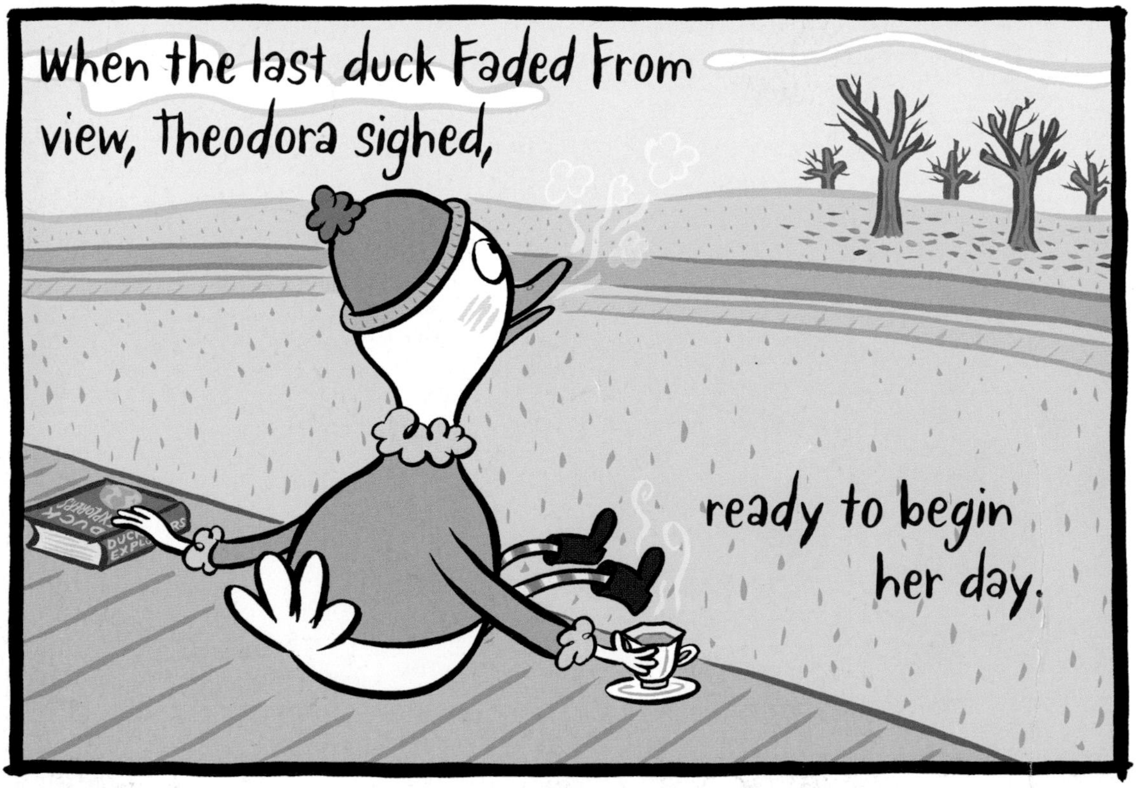
When the last duck faded from view, Theodora sighed,
ready to begin her day.

then she noticed something unusual . . .

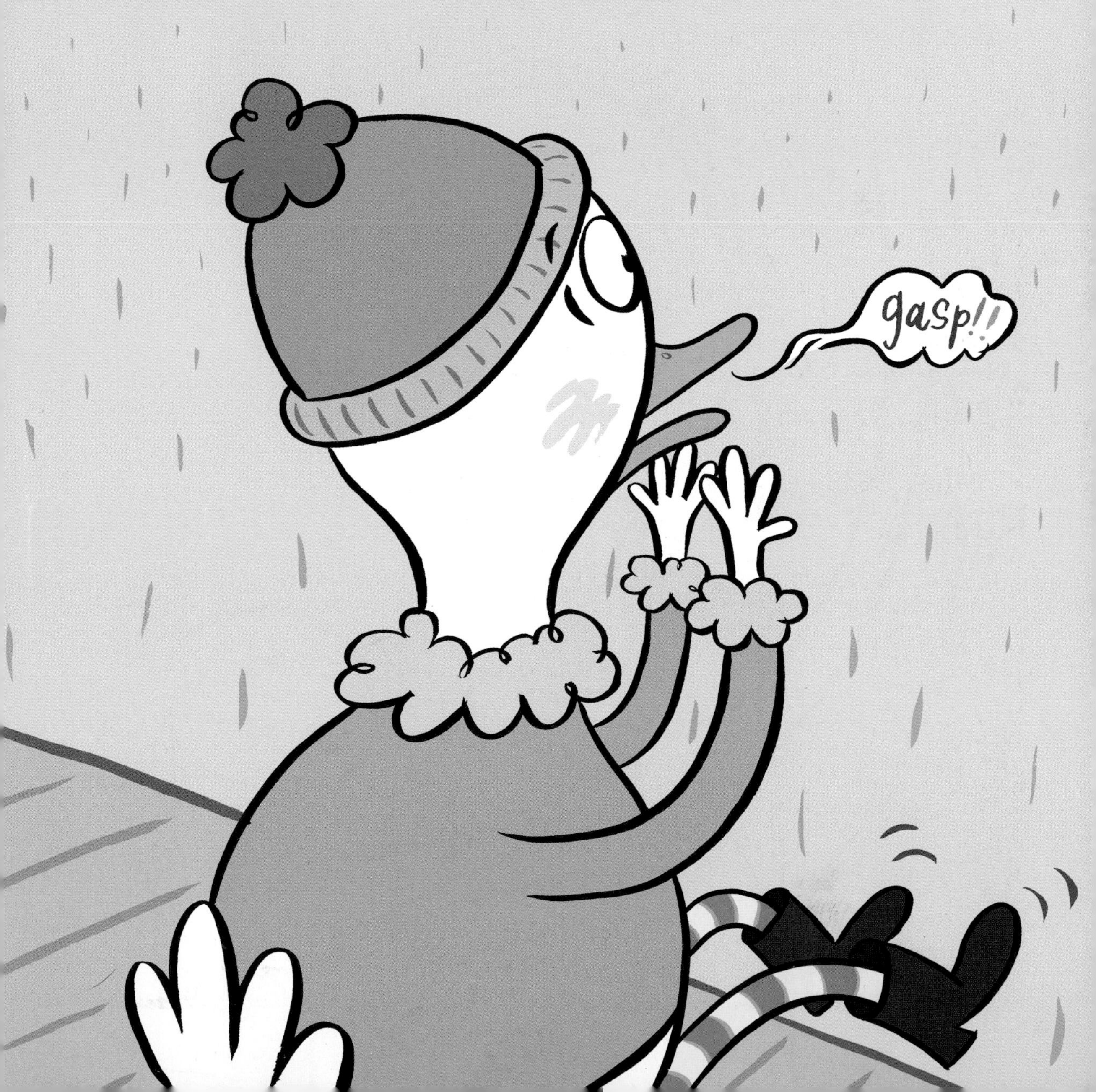
gasp!!

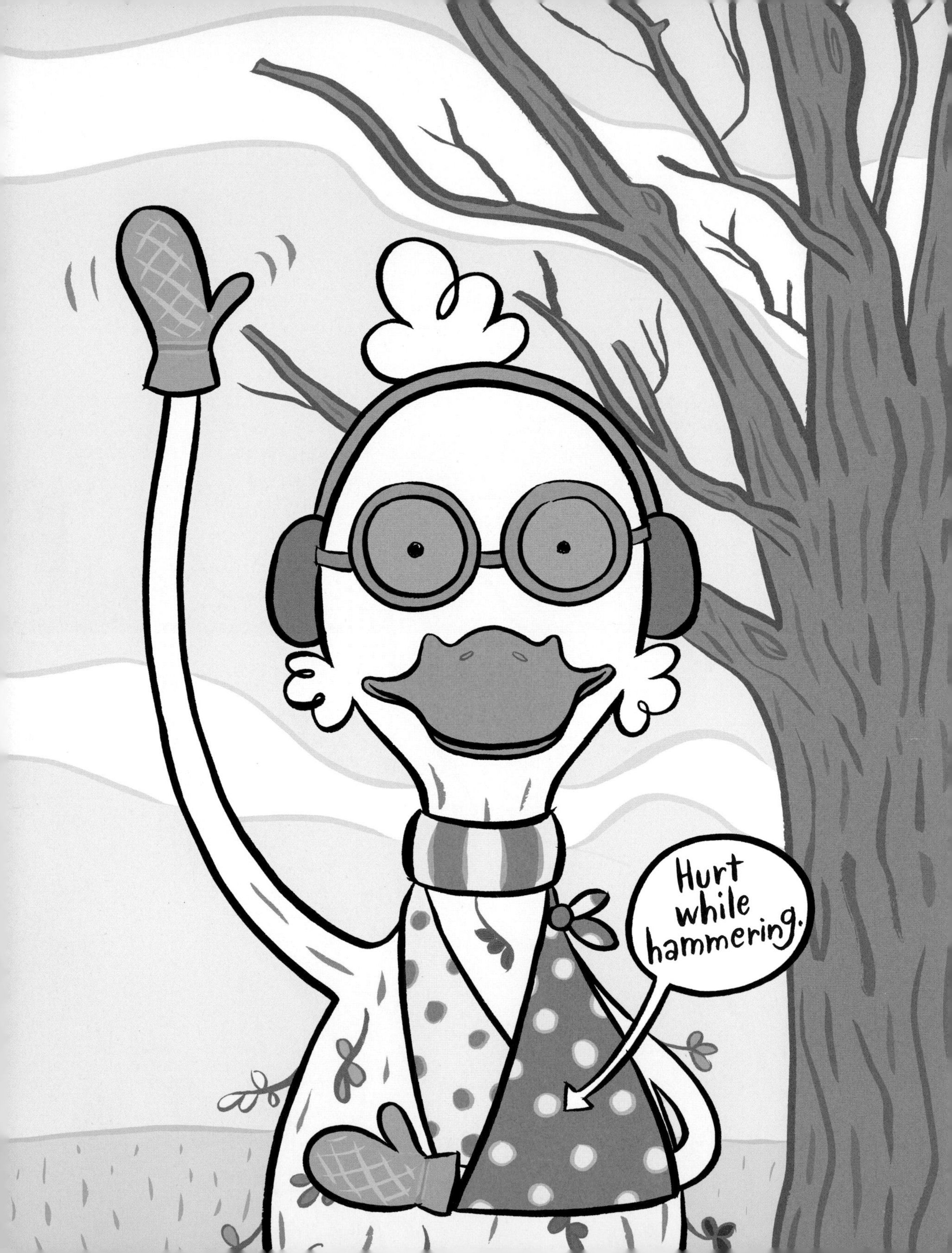
Hurt while hammering.

CHAD!!!

In winter, every morning, Theodora would do her duck exercises in the warmth and safety of her bathtub.

CHAPTER

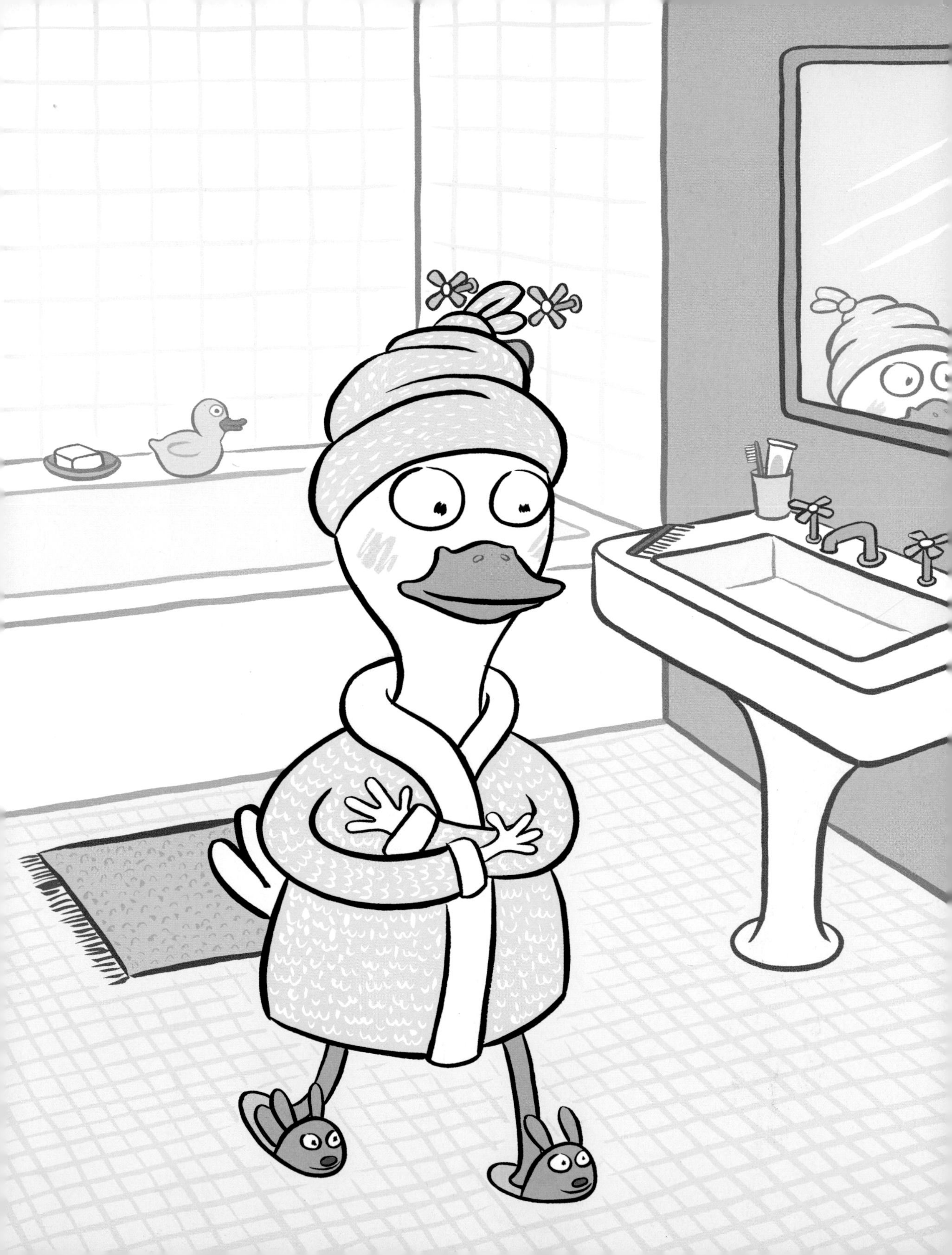

But not Chad.
He did not seem to notice the cold at all.

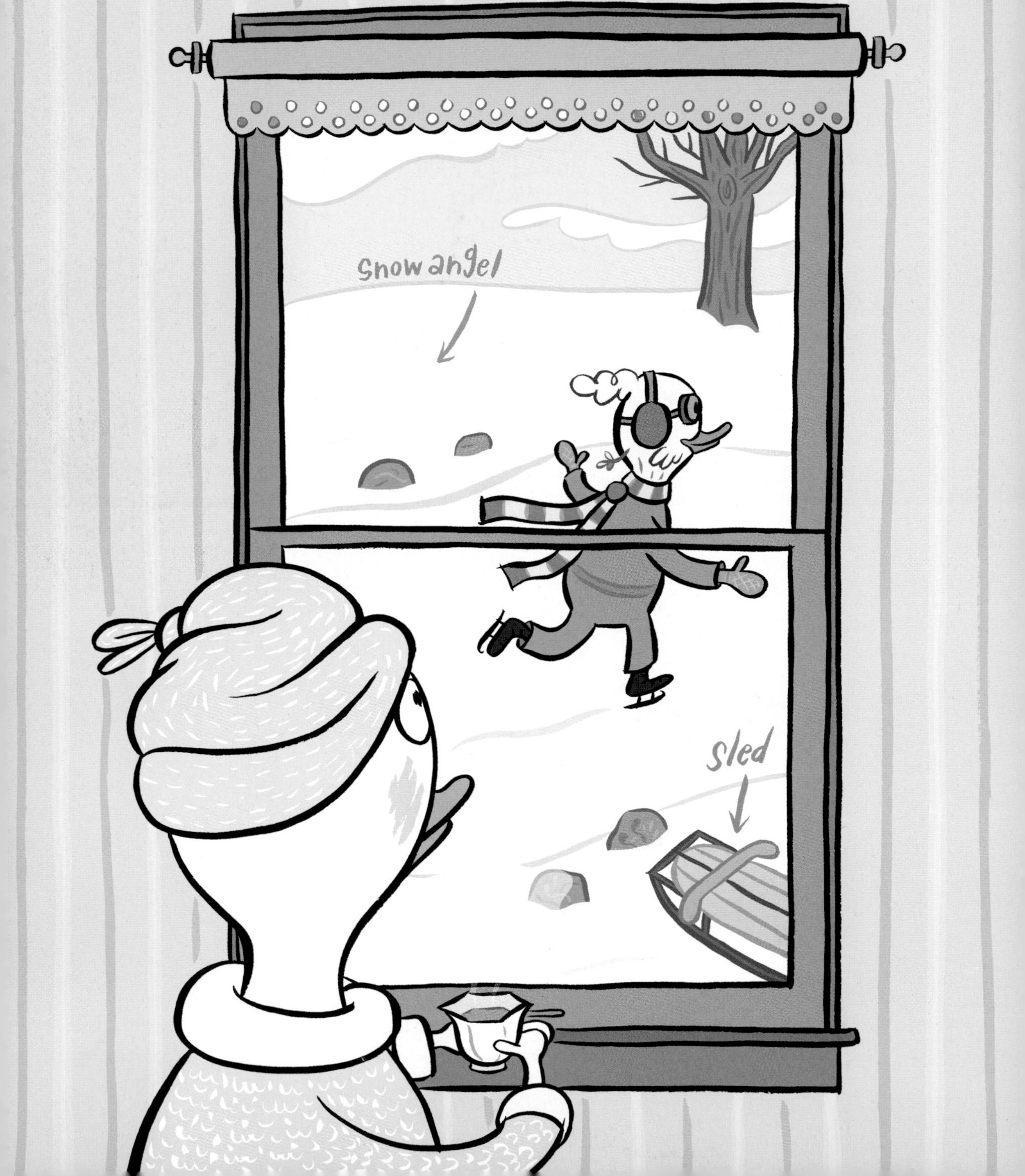
snow angel
sled

theodora would brave the winter cold only once each day, when she stepped outside to look up at the night stars.

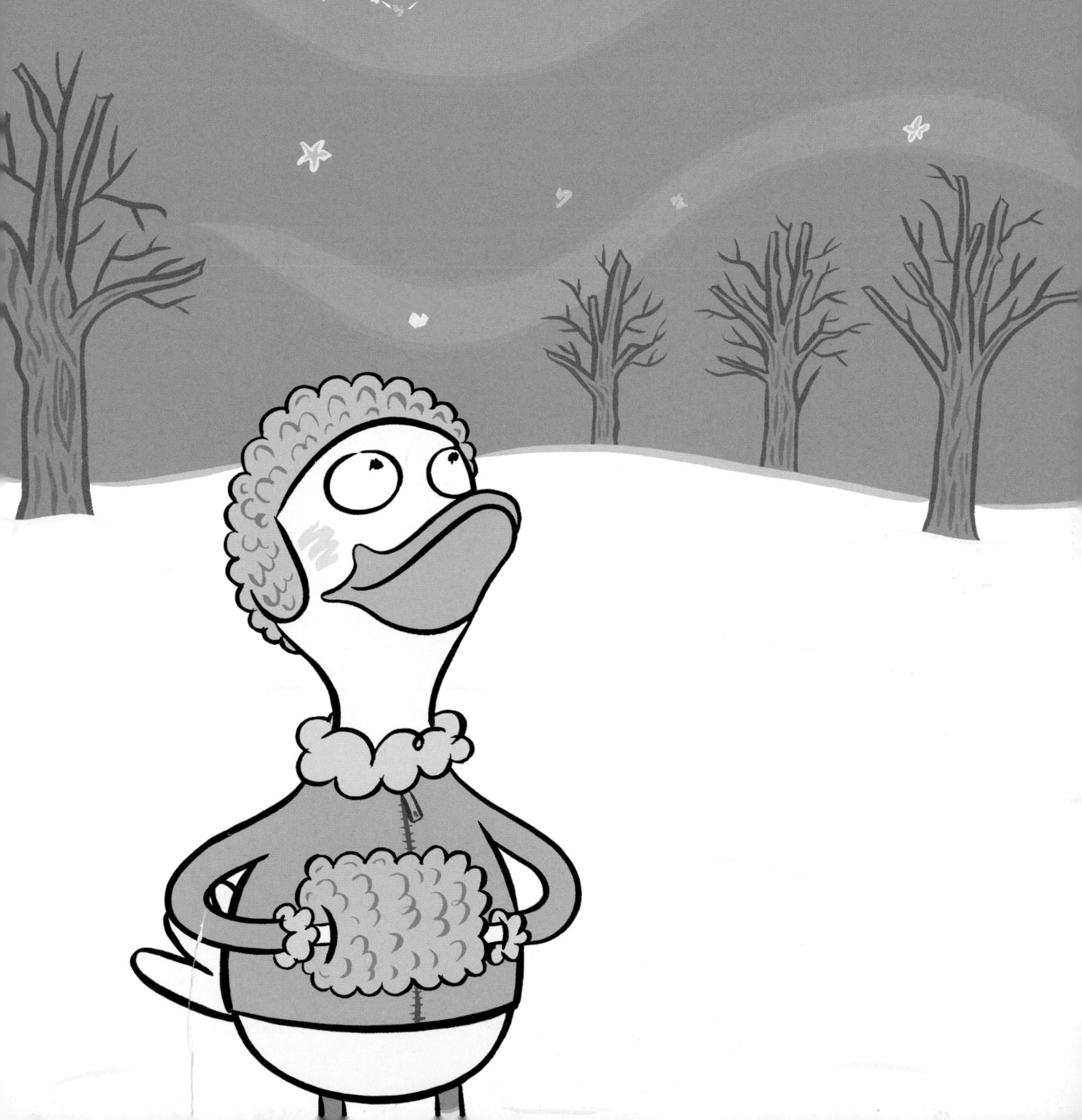

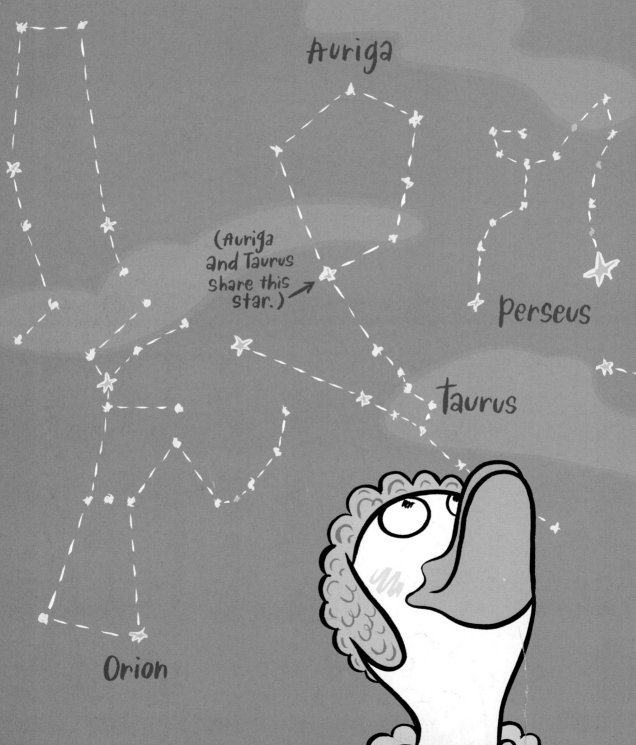

Gemini

↑
(North)

Auriga

Perseus

(Auriga
and Taurus
share this
star.) →

Taurus

Orion

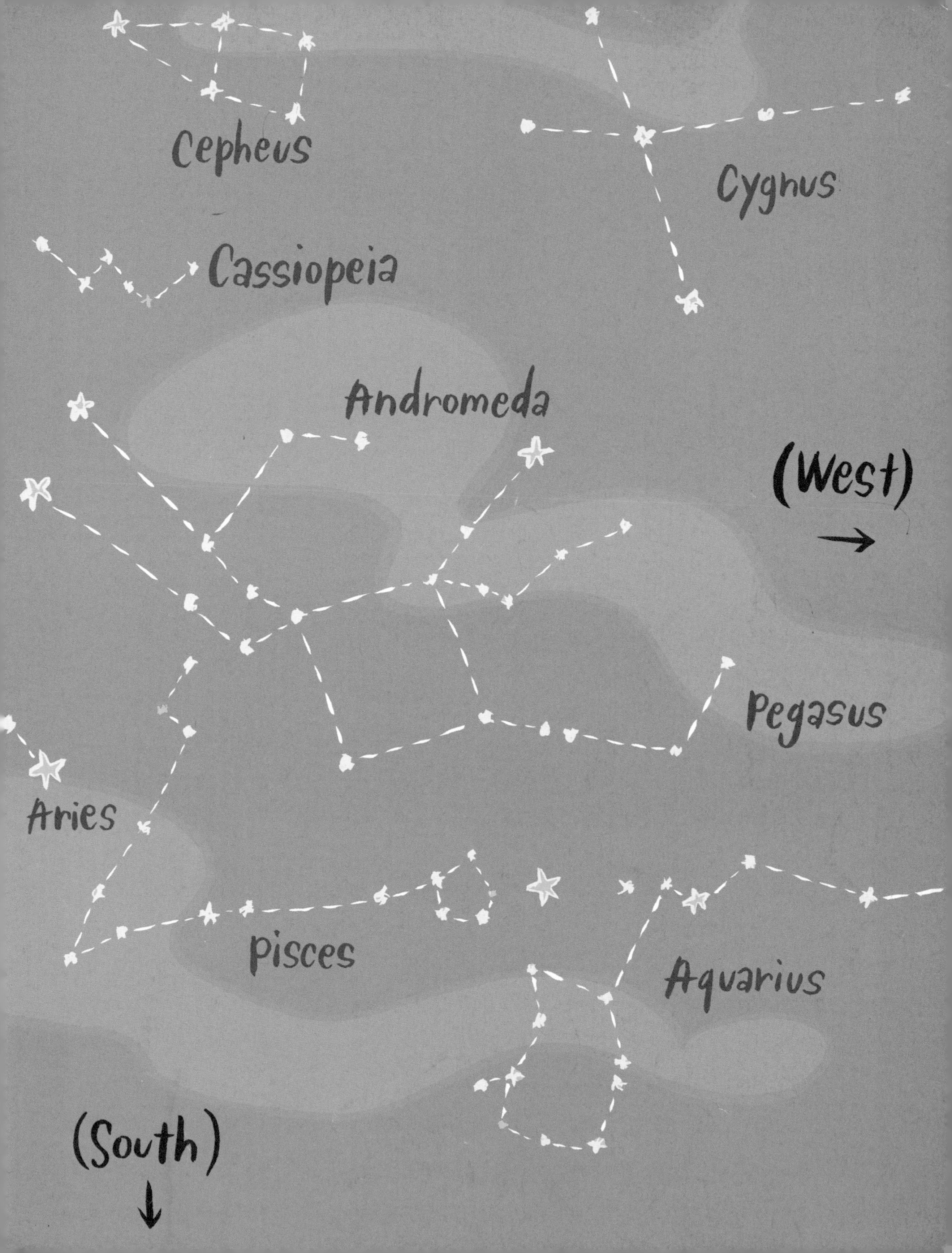
Cepheus
Cygnus
Cassiopeia
Andromeda
(West)
Pegasus
Aries
Pisces
Aquarius
(South)

"Would you like to look through my telescope?" she heard Chad call.

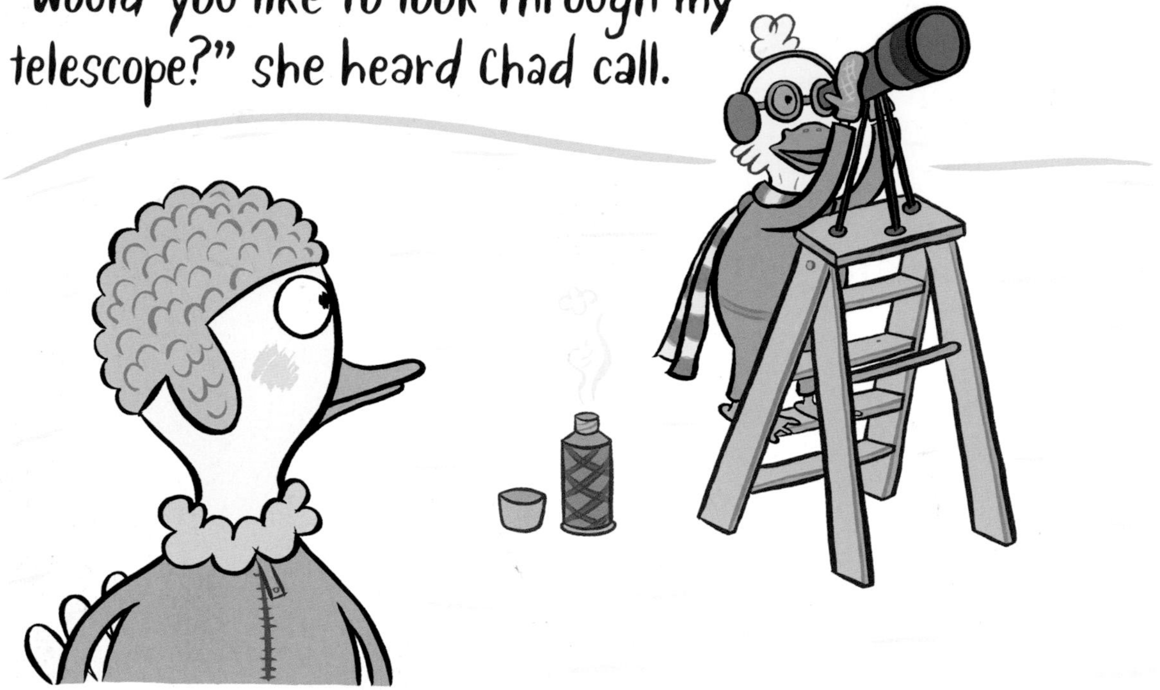

"Here, take a look."

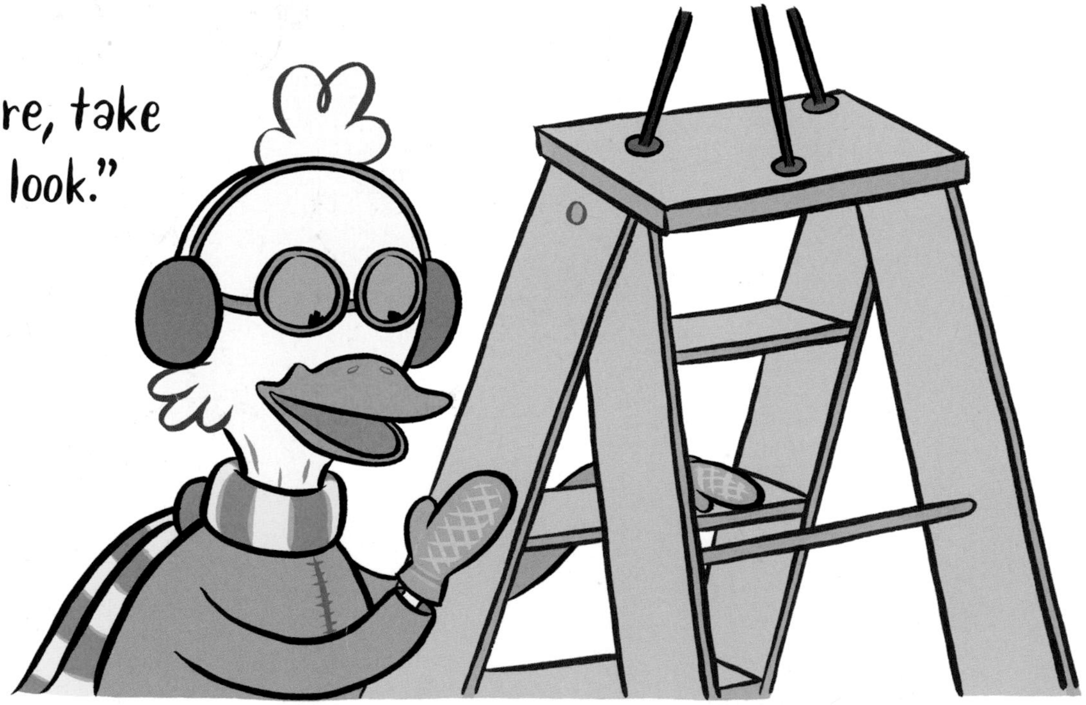

Being a well-mannered duck, Theodora could not refuse.

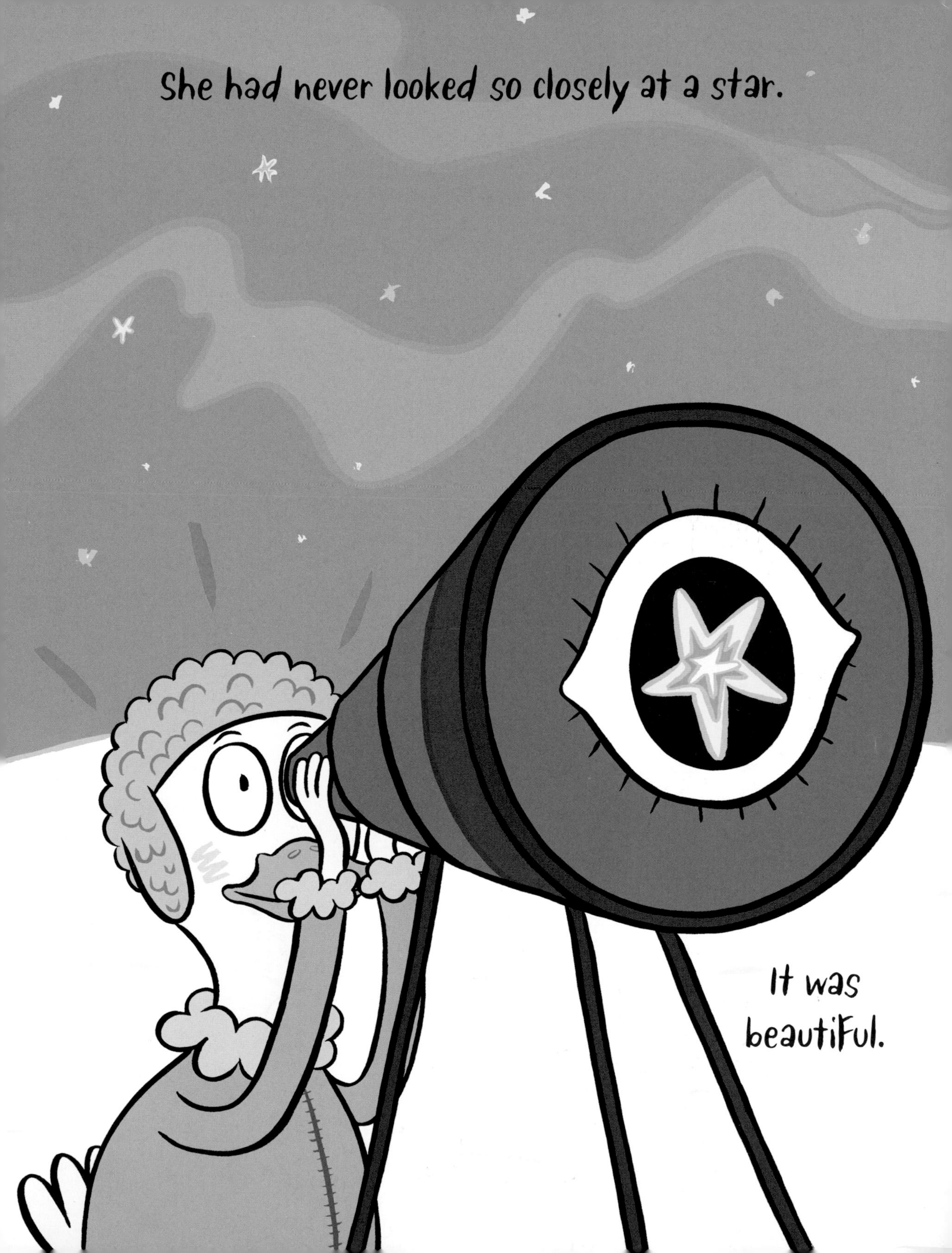
She had never looked so closely at a star.
It was beautiful.

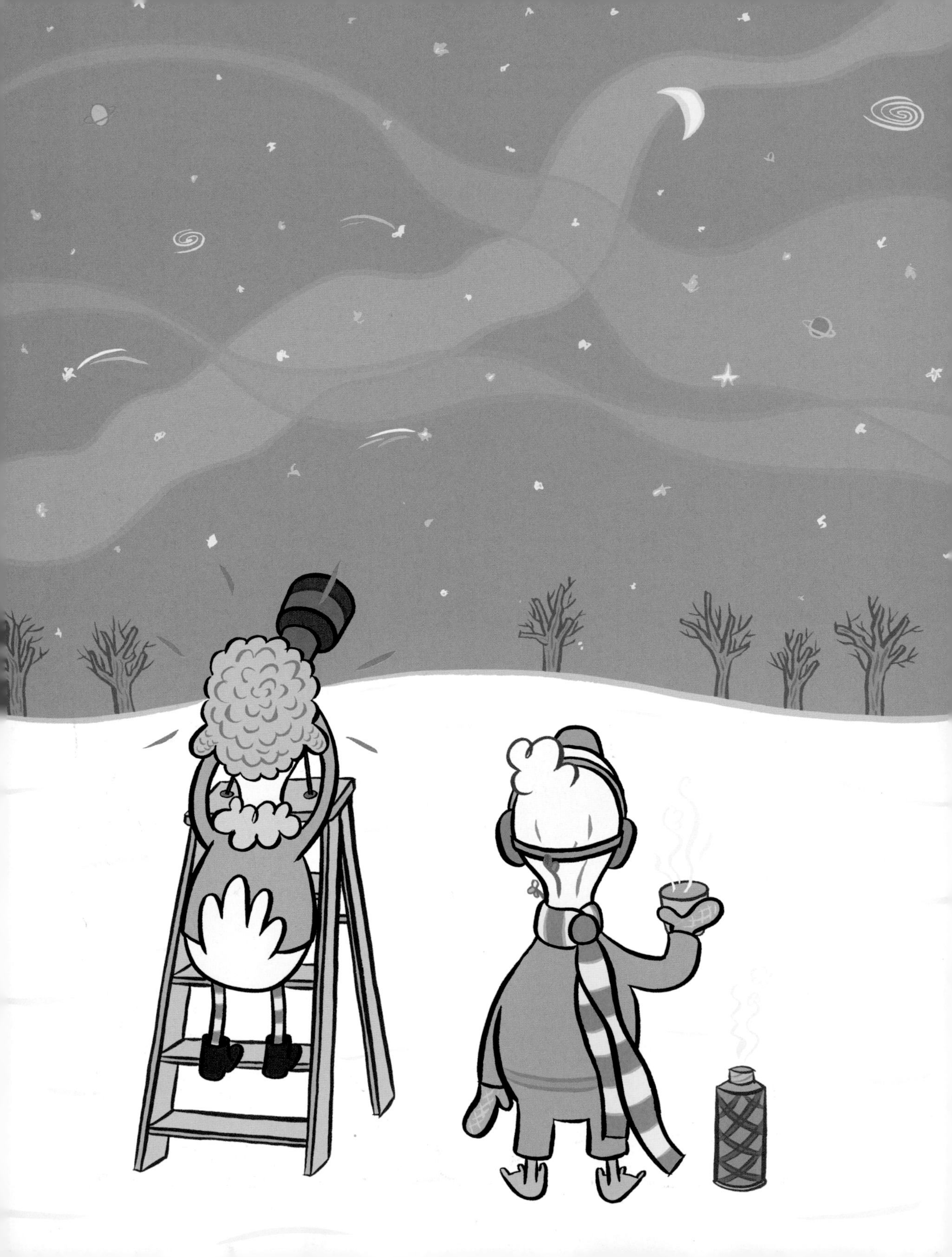

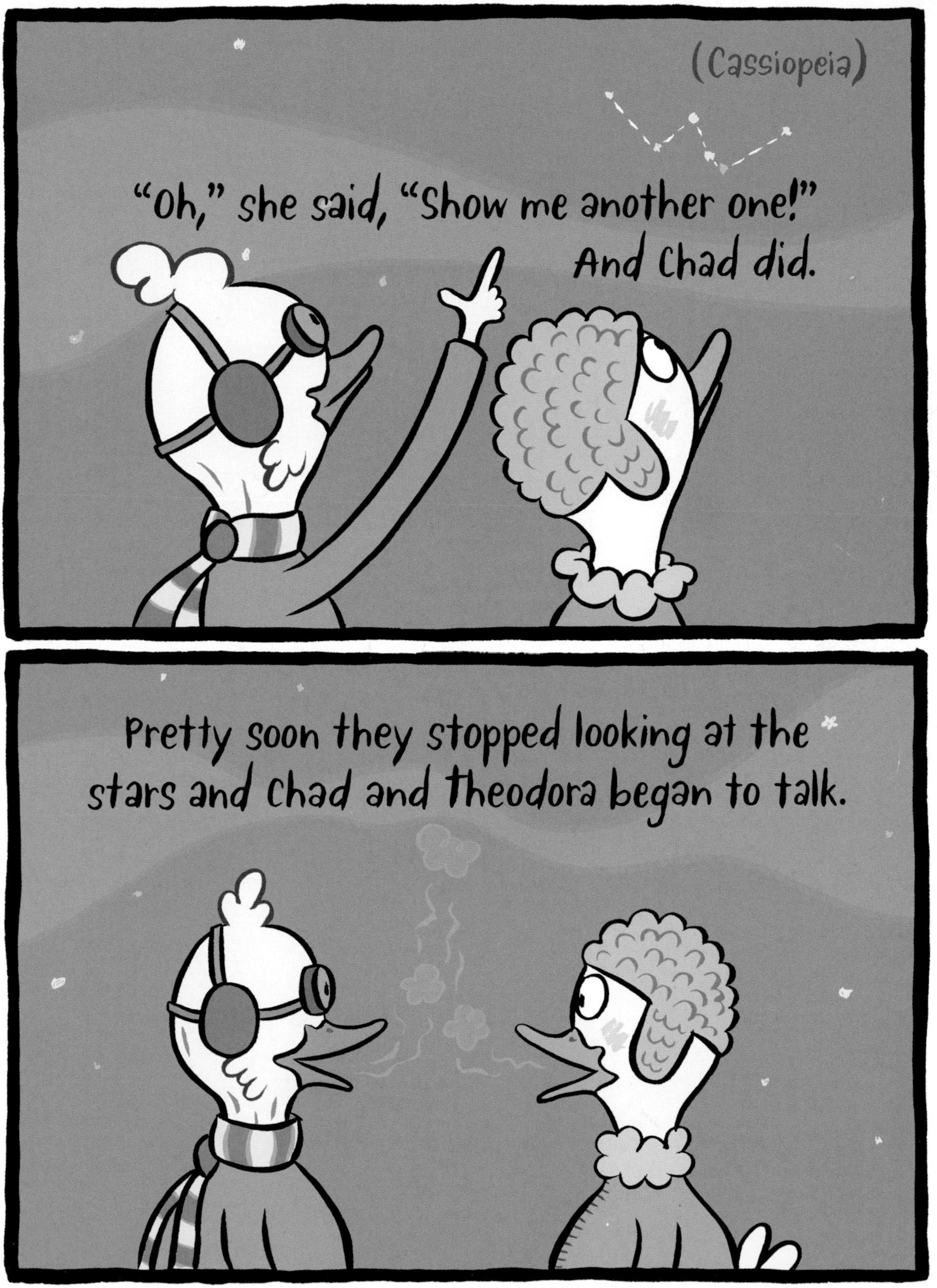
(Cassiopeia)
"Oh," she said, "Show me another one!"
And Chad did.
Pretty soon they stopped looking at the stars and Chad and Theodora began to talk.

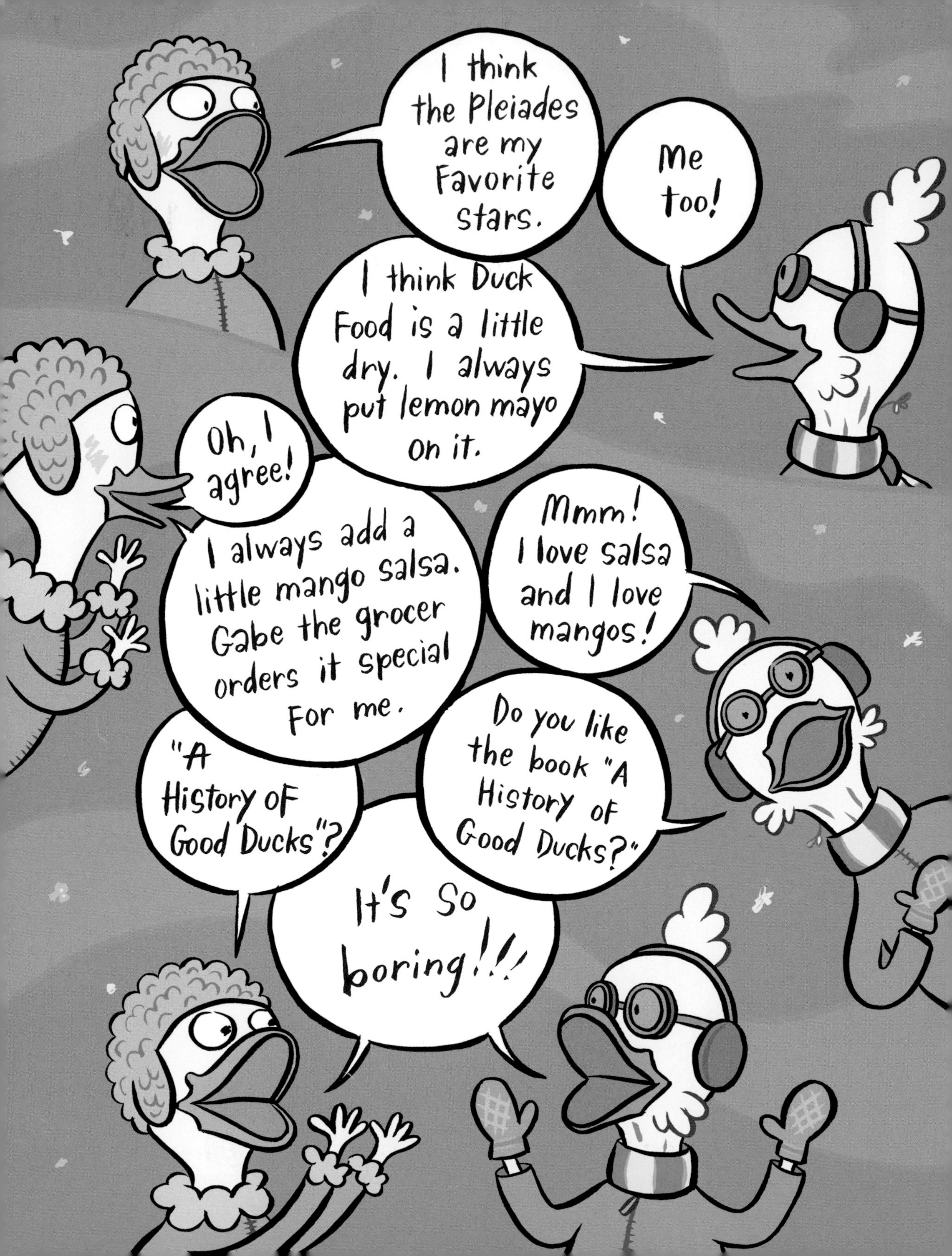
I think the Pleiades are my Favorite stars.
Me too!
I think Duck Food is a little dry. I always put lemon mayo on it.
Oh, I agree!
I always add a little mango salsa. Gabe the grocer orders it special For me.
Mmm! I love salsa and I love mangos!
Do you like the book "A History of Good Ducks?"
"A History of Good Ducks"?
It's so boring!!!

Maybe chad was not so bad after all.

CHAPTER

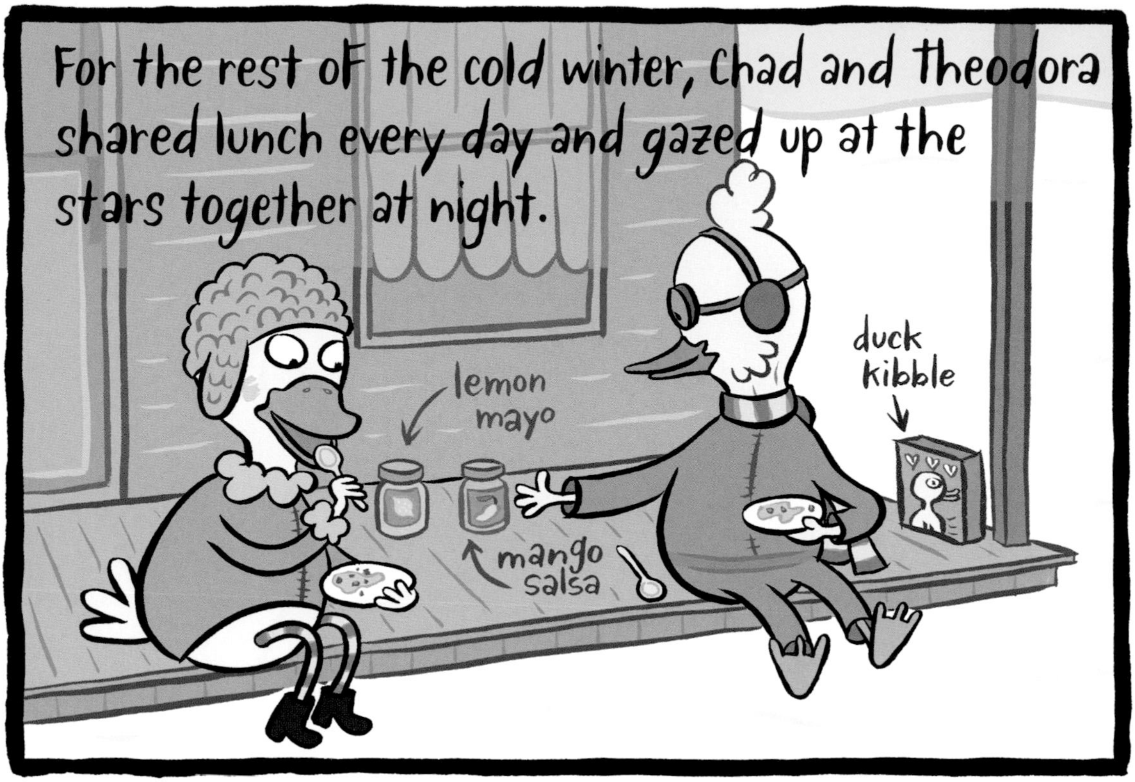
For the rest of the cold winter, Chad and Theodora shared lunch every day and gazed up at the stars together at night.
lemon mayo
mango salsa
duck kibble

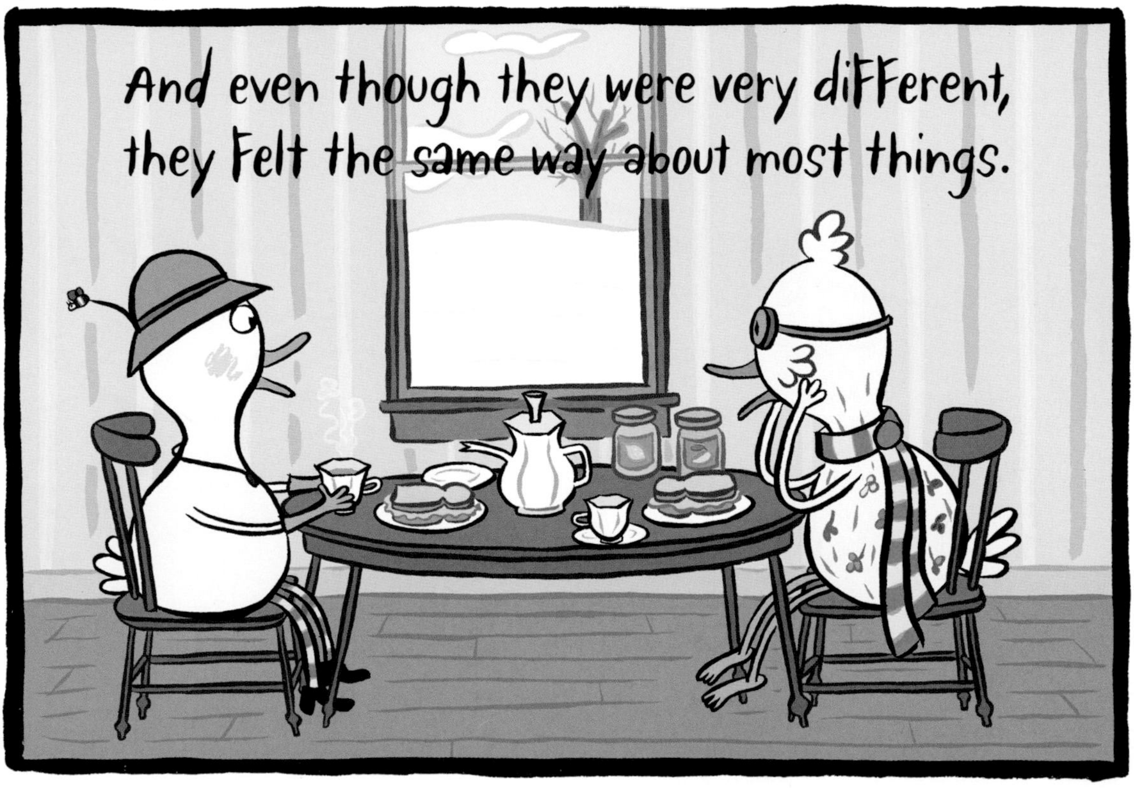
And even though they were very different, they felt the same way about most things.

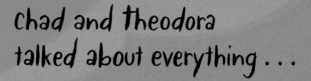

Chad and Theodora
talked about everything . . .

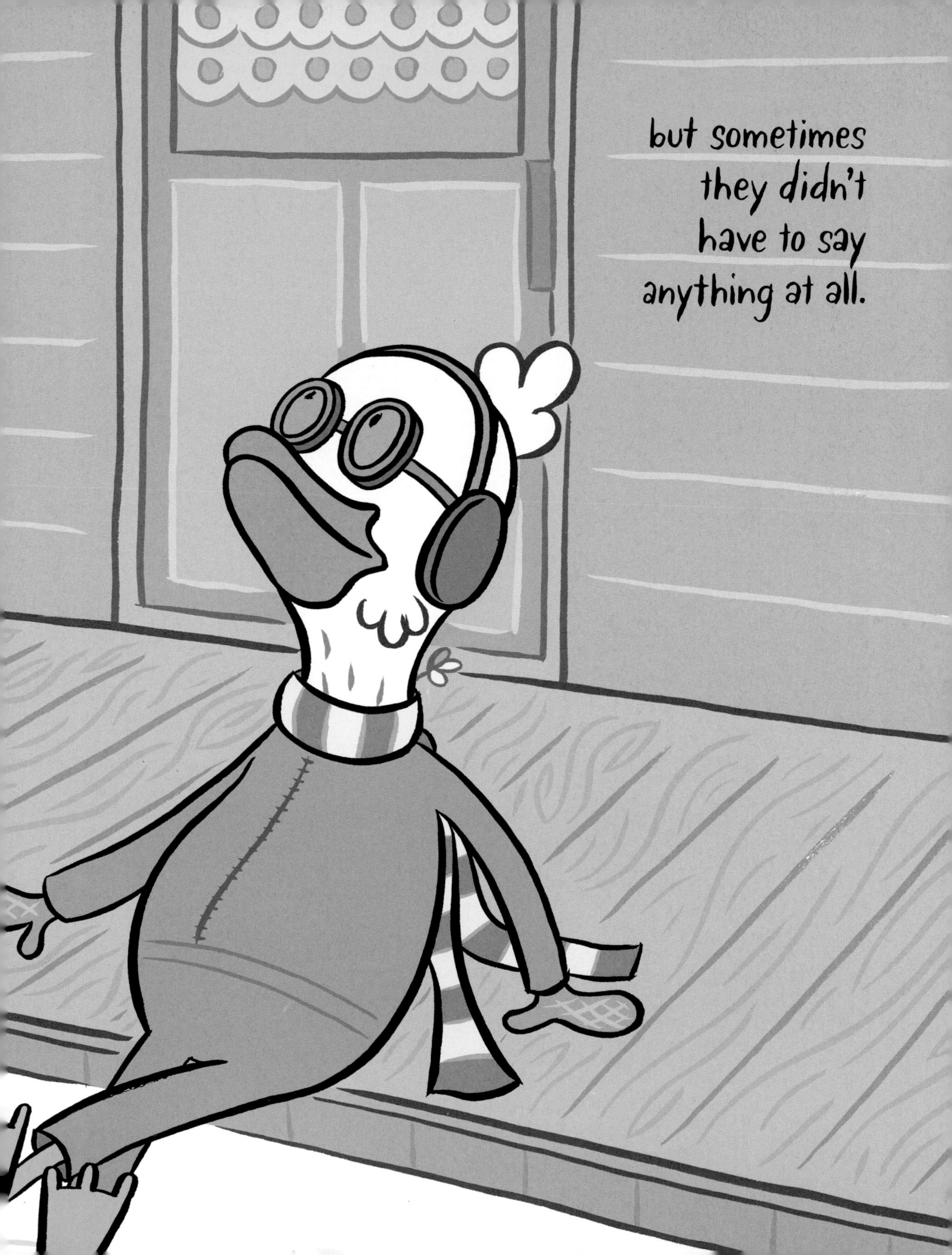

but sometimes
they didn't
have to say
anything at all.

By the time the other ducks came back from their trip south, Theodora and Chad were inseparable.

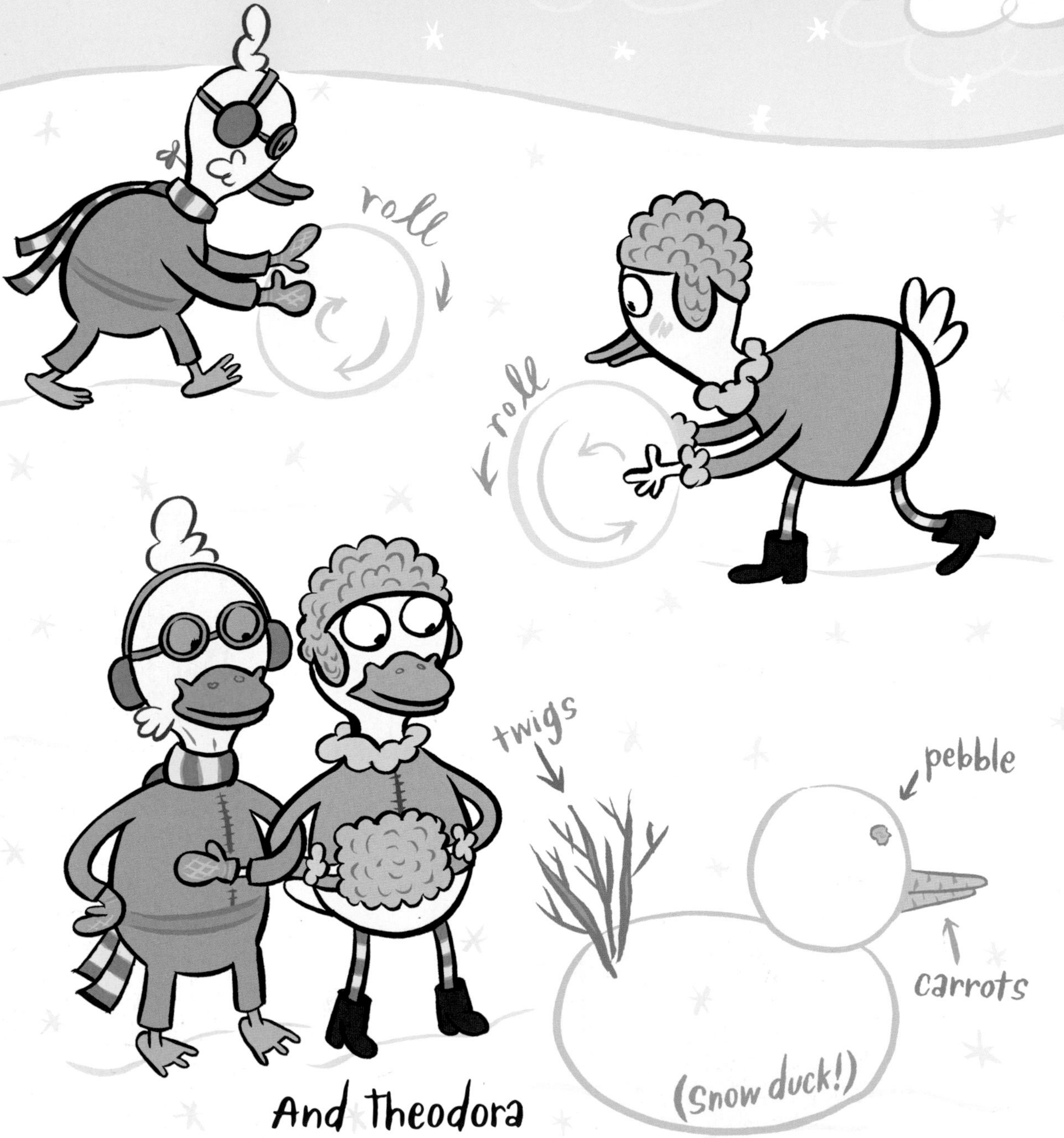
roll
roll
twigs
pebble
carrots
(snow duck!)

And Theodora had something she never had before.

theodora had a best Friend.

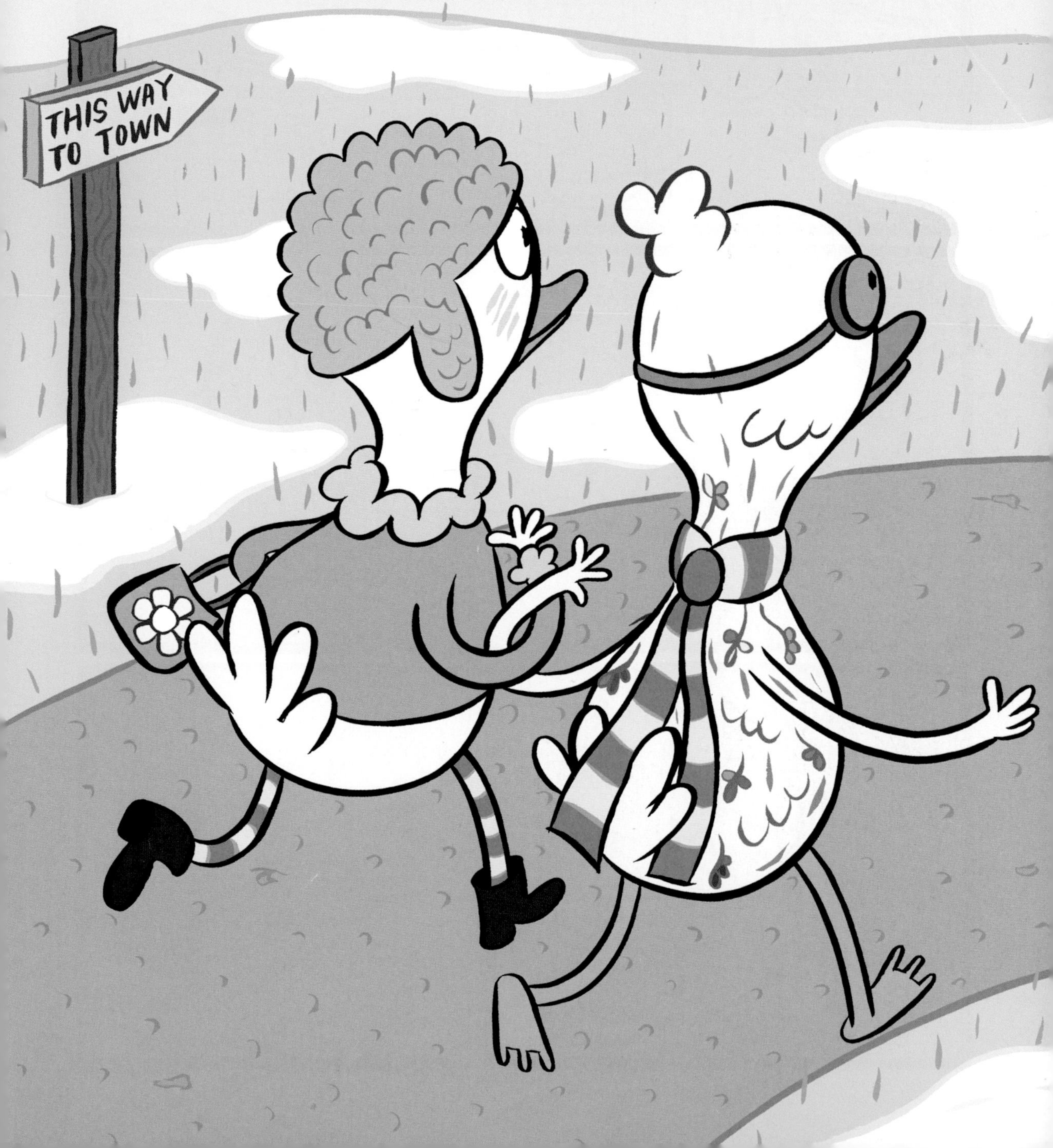
THIS WAY
TO TOWN

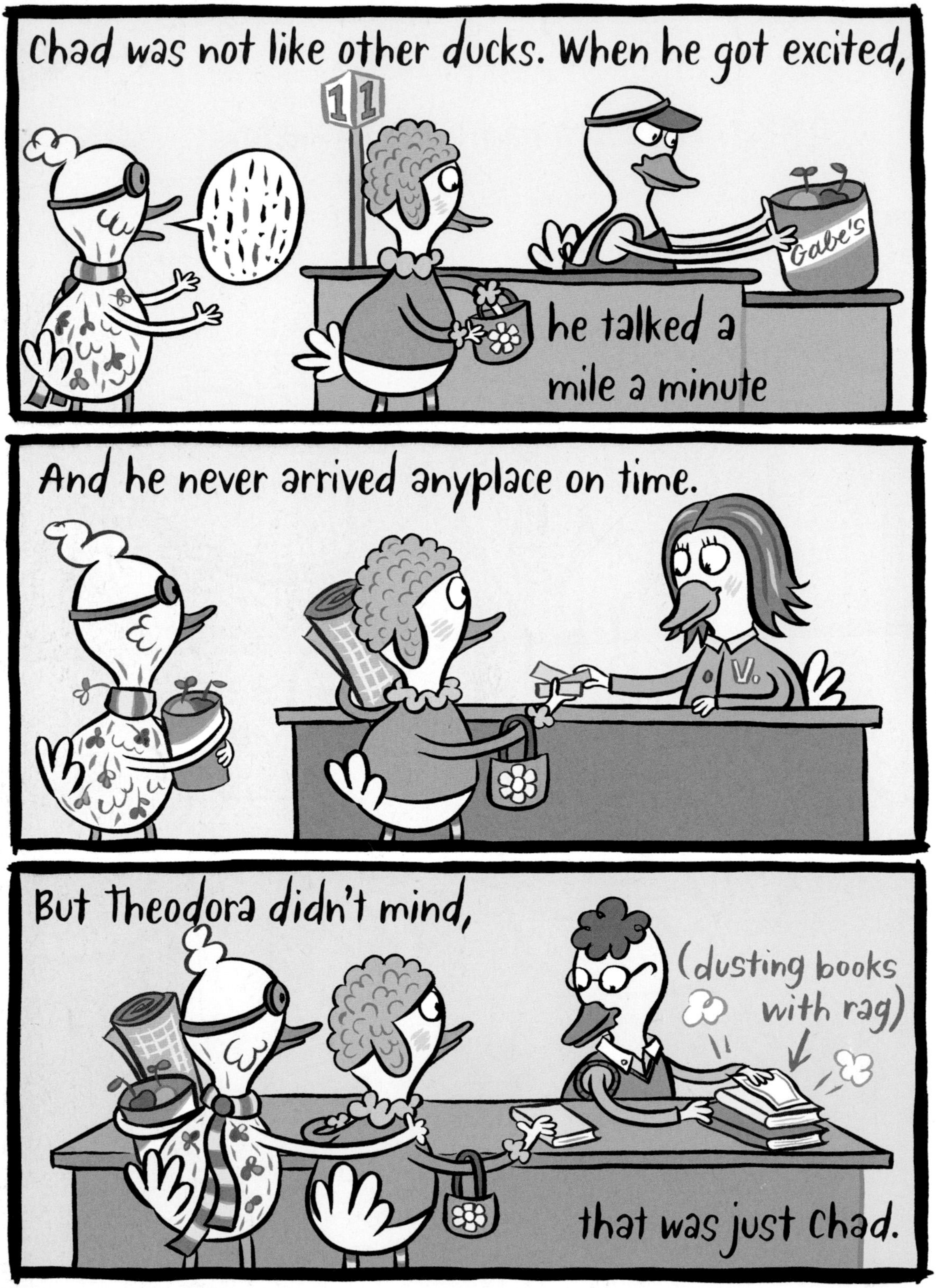
Chad was not like other ducks. When he got excited,
11
Gabe's
he talked a mile a minute
And he never arrived anyplace on time.
V.
But Theodora didn't mind,
(dusting books with rag)
that was just Chad.

One day when they were walking back through town after doing errands, Theodora and Chad overheard Gabe, Velma, and Maxwell snickering.

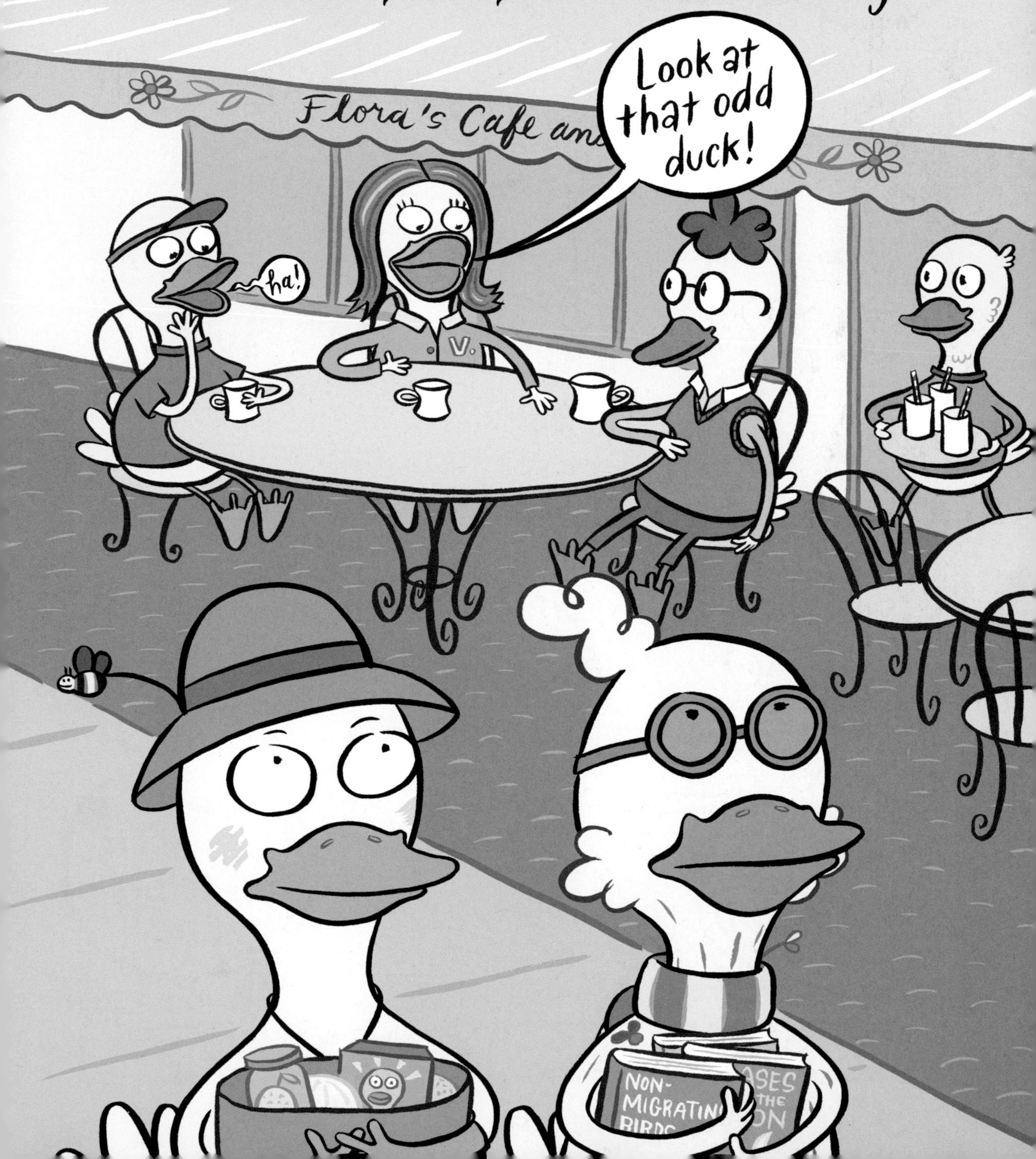
Flora's Cafe
ha!
Look at that odd duck!
V.
NON-

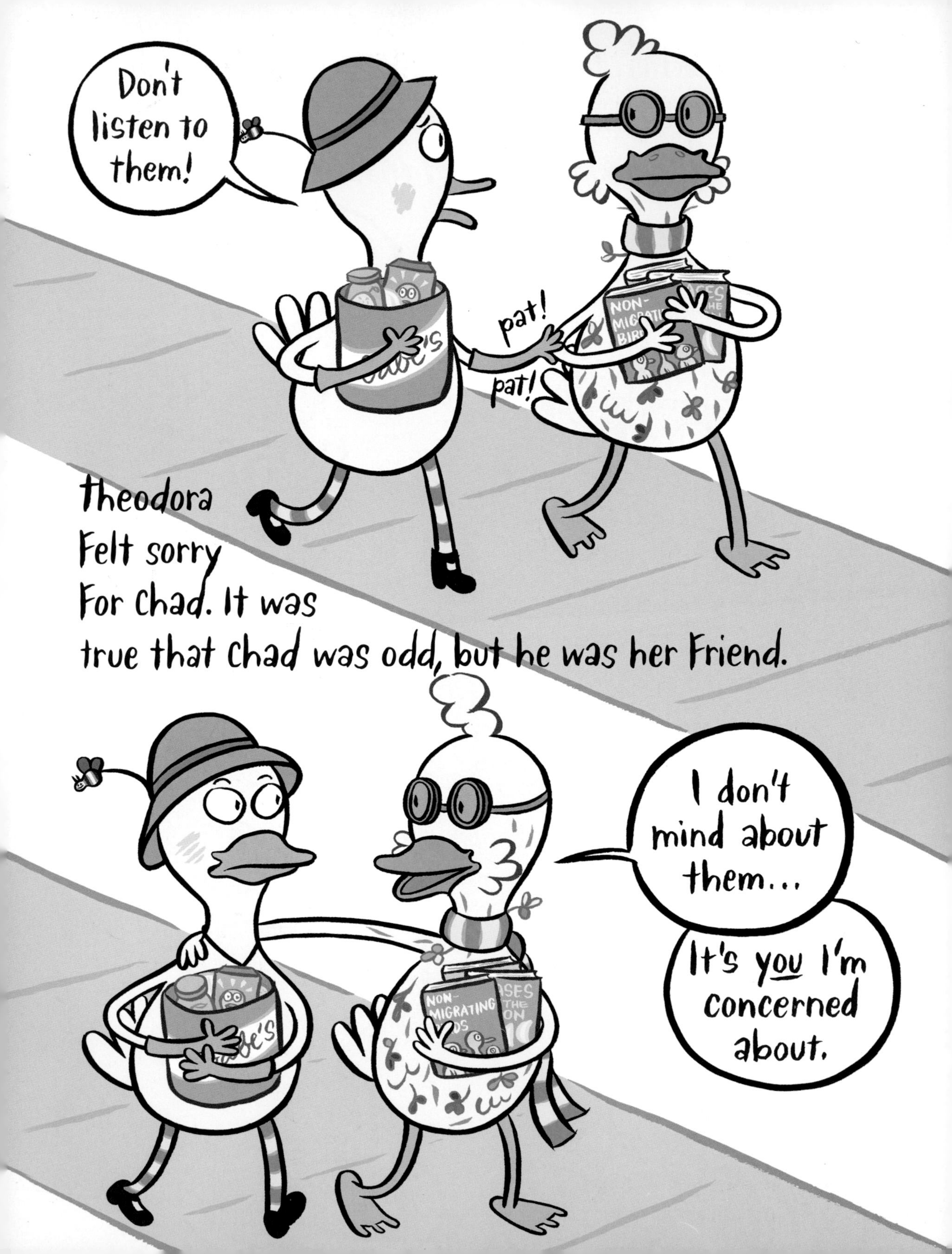
Don't listen to them!
pat!
pat!
theodora Felt sorry For Chad. It was true that Chad was odd, but he was her Friend.
I don't mind about them...
It's you I'm concerned about.

Don't be concerned For me!
Yes, those ducks are right!
I'm not odd, you're odd!!
Well, it's just that we have to Face it. Those ducks are right.
you are a bit odd.
they were calling you the odd duck!!
NON-
Gabe's

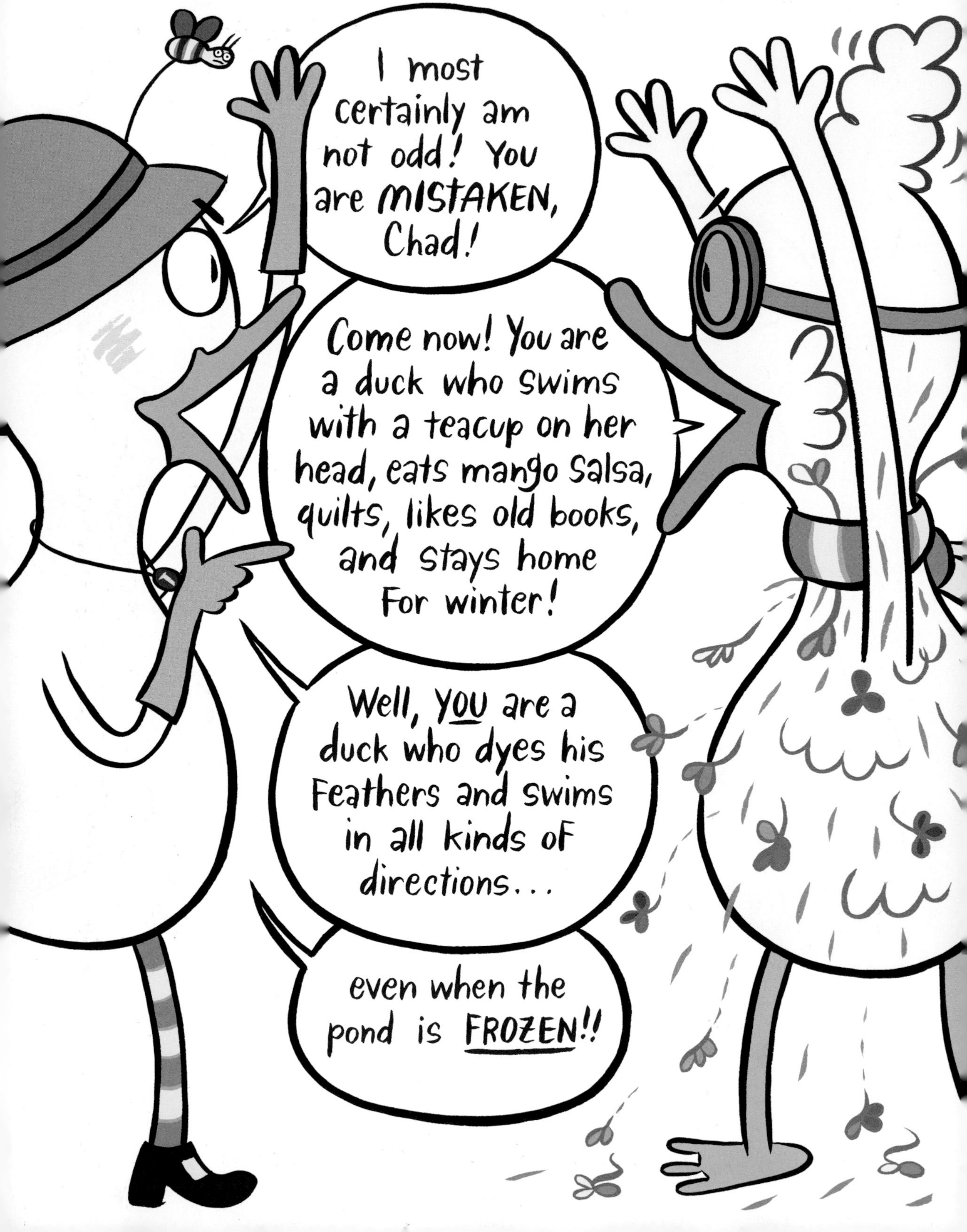
I most certainly am not odd! You are MISTAKEN, Chad!
Come now! You are a duck who swims with a teacup on her head, eats mango salsa, quilts, likes old books, and stays home for winter!
Well, YOU are a duck who dyes his feathers and swims in all kinds of directions...
even when the pond is FROZEN!!

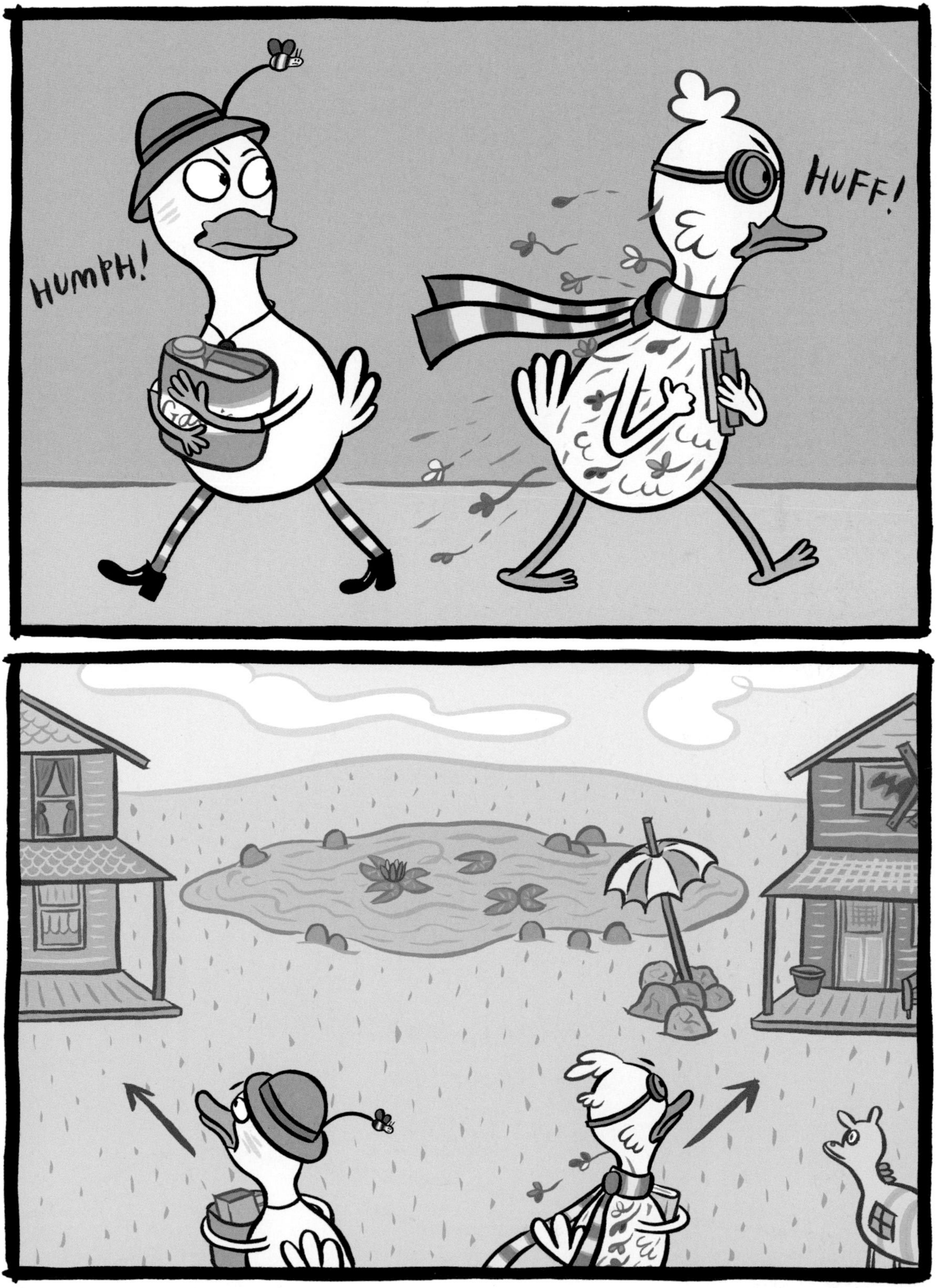
HUMPH!
HUFF!

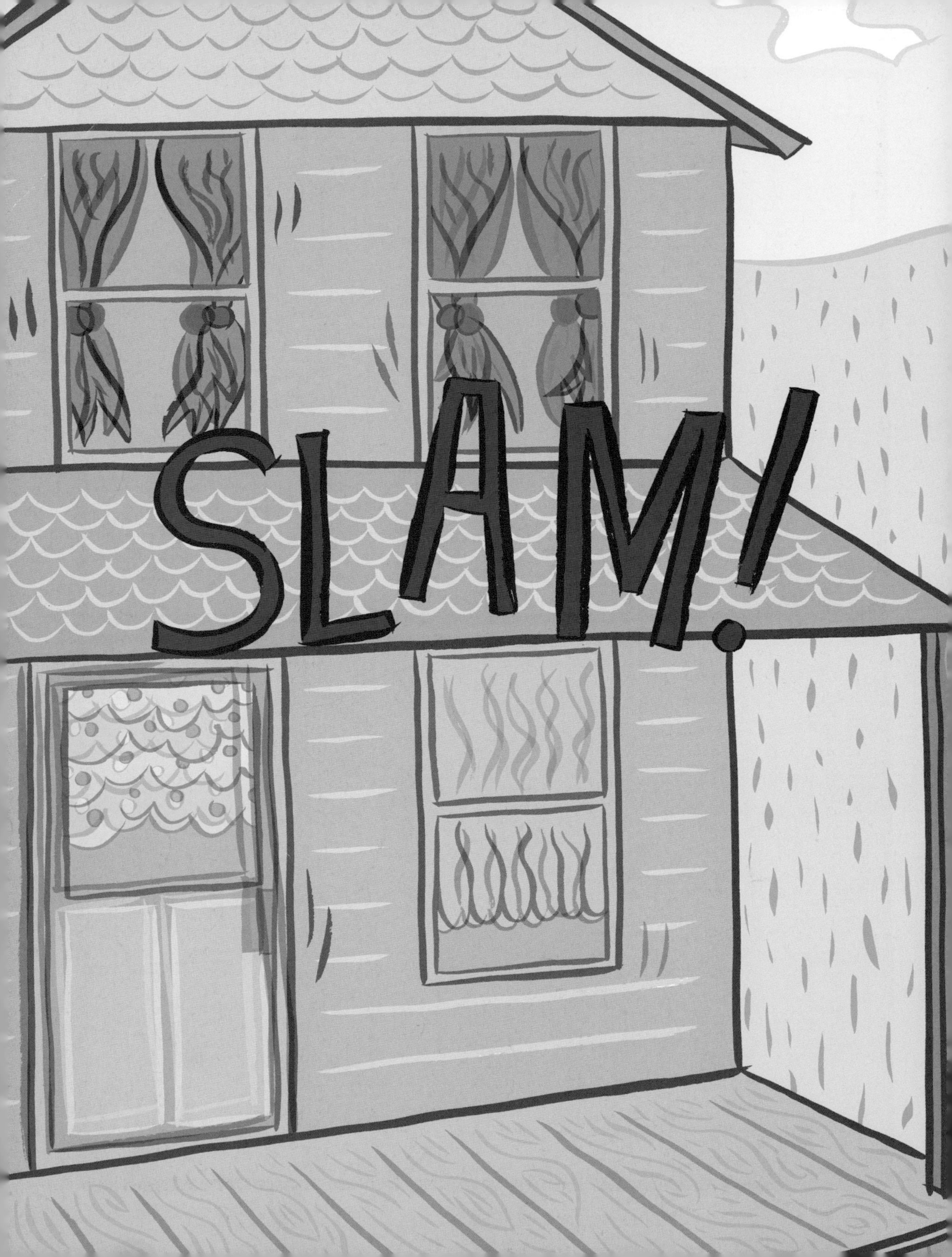
SLAM!

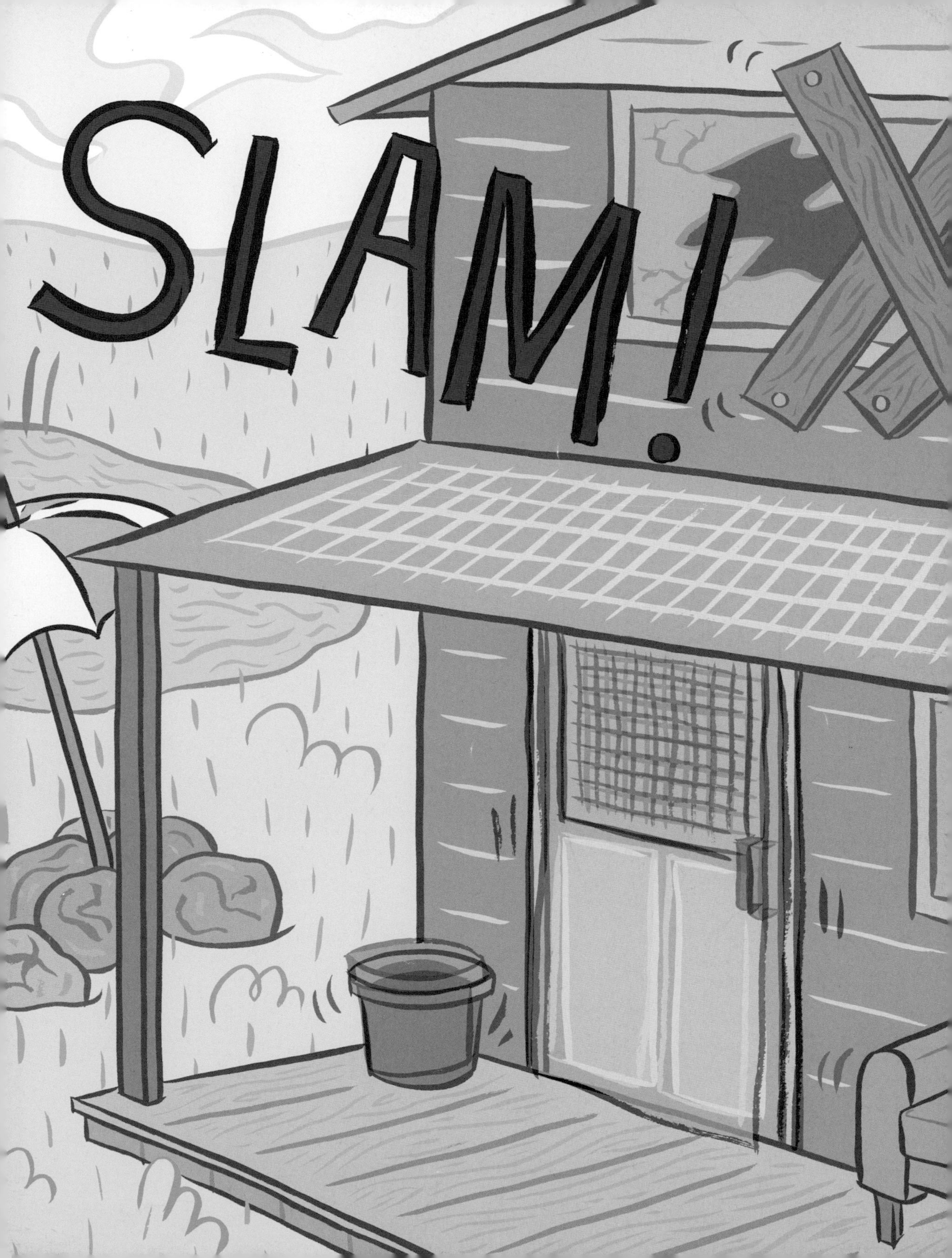
SLAM!

CHAPTER

6

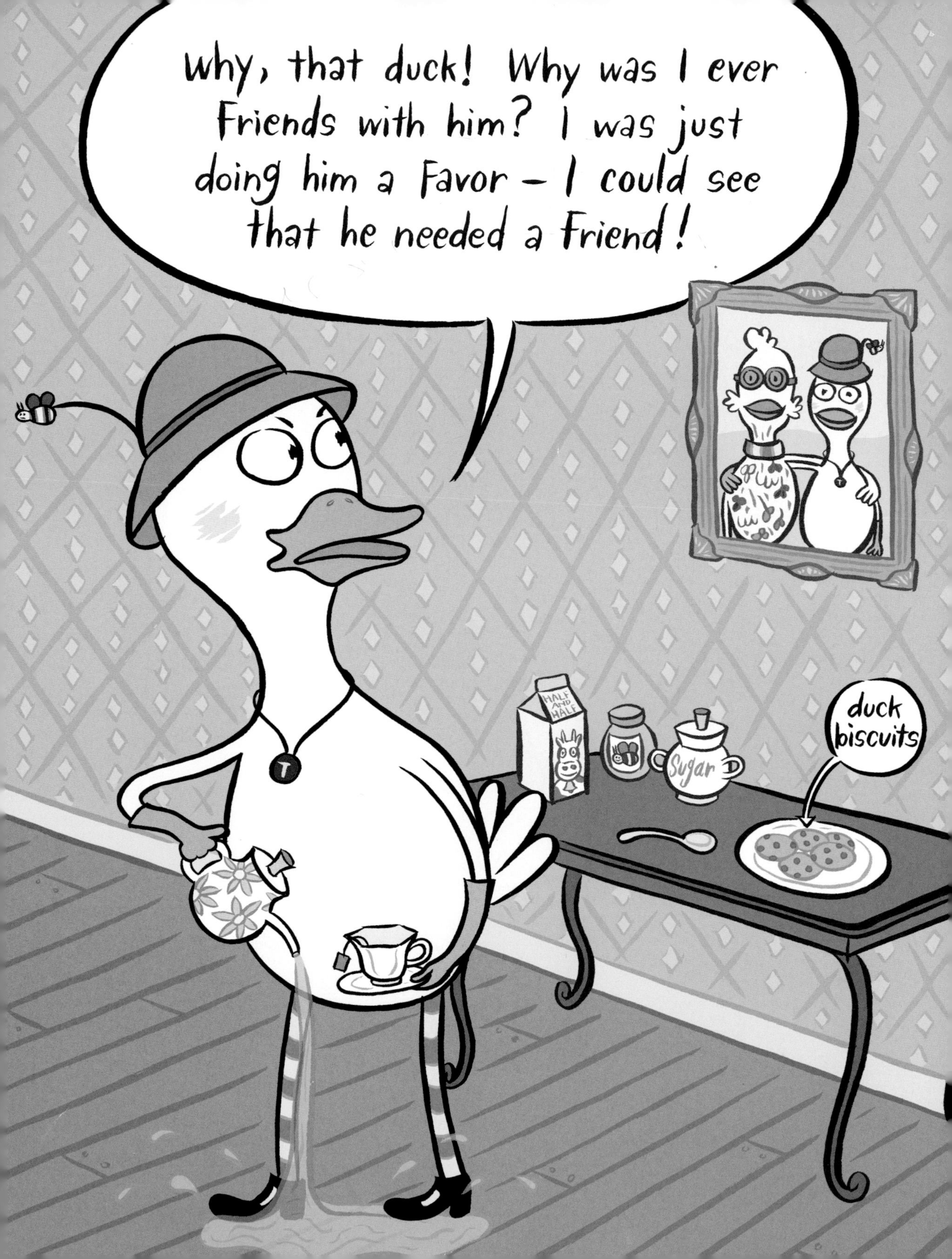
Why, that duck! Why was I ever Friends with him? I was just doing him a Favor – I could see that he needed a Friend!
HALF AND HALF
Sugar
duck biscuits

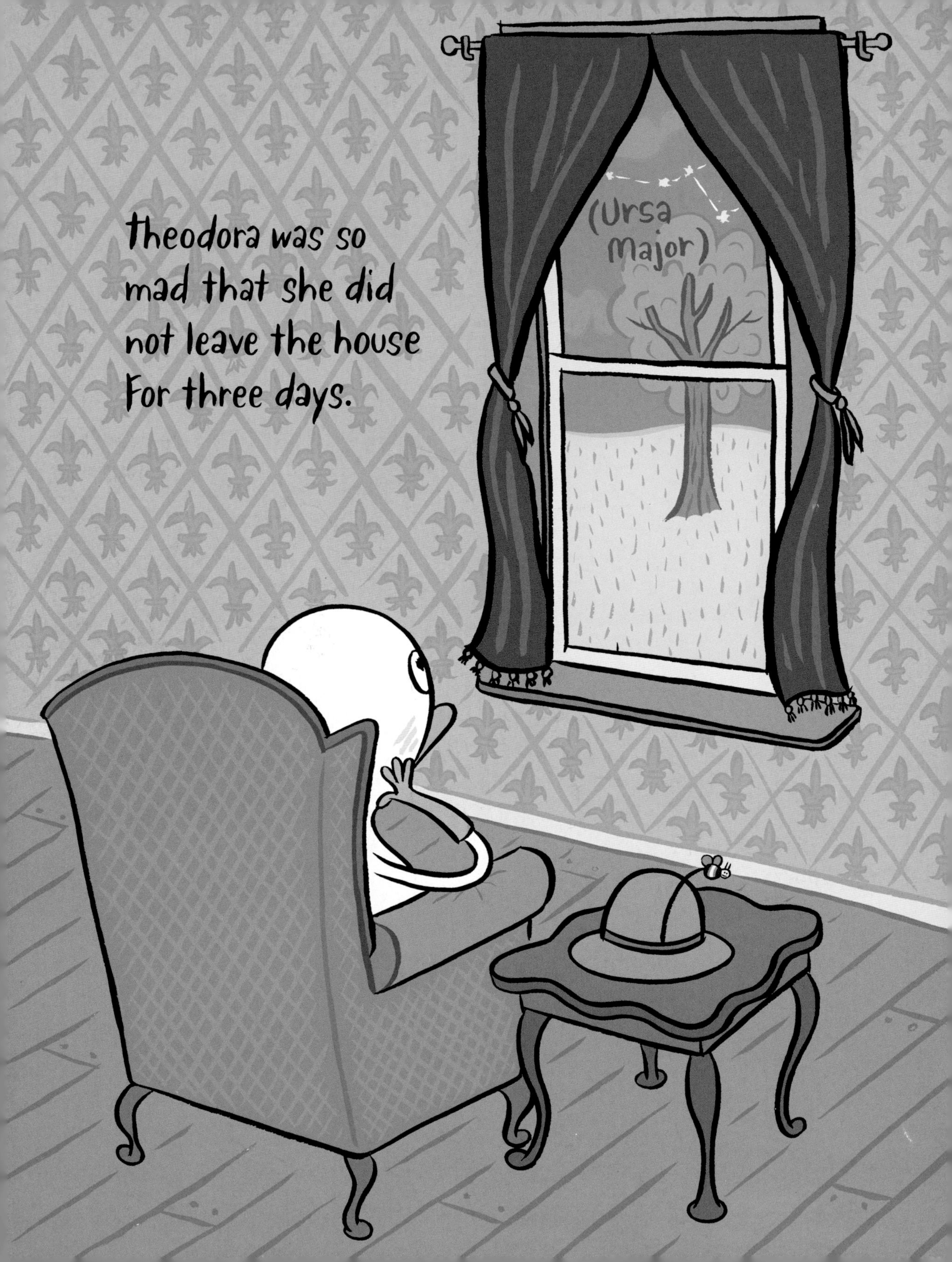
theodora was so mad that she did not leave the house for three days.
(Ursa Major)

She did not like being angry. It made her uncomfortable. Not even rose hip tea could calm her down.

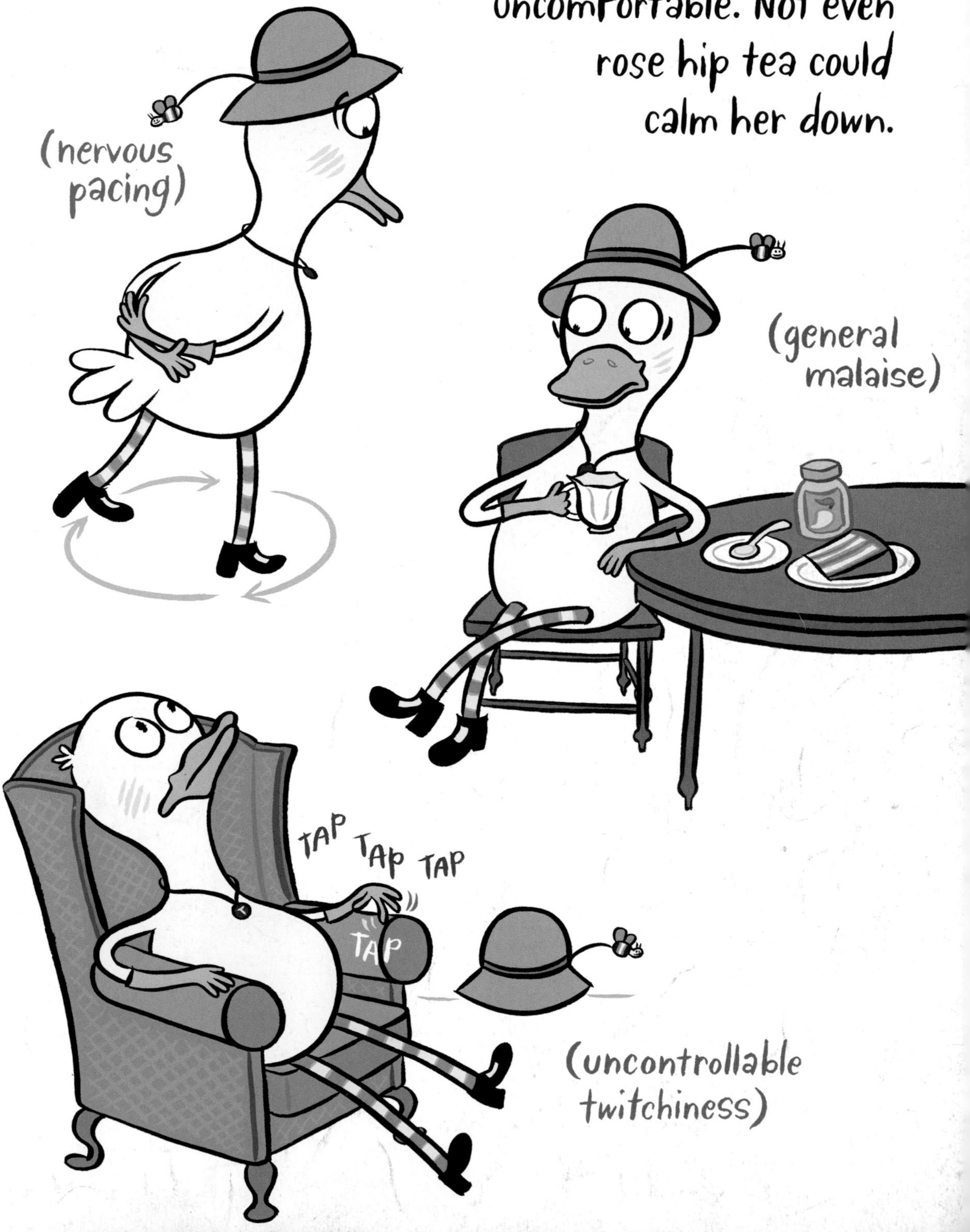
(nervous pacing)
(general malaise)
TAP TAP TAP
TAP
(uncontrollable twitchiness)

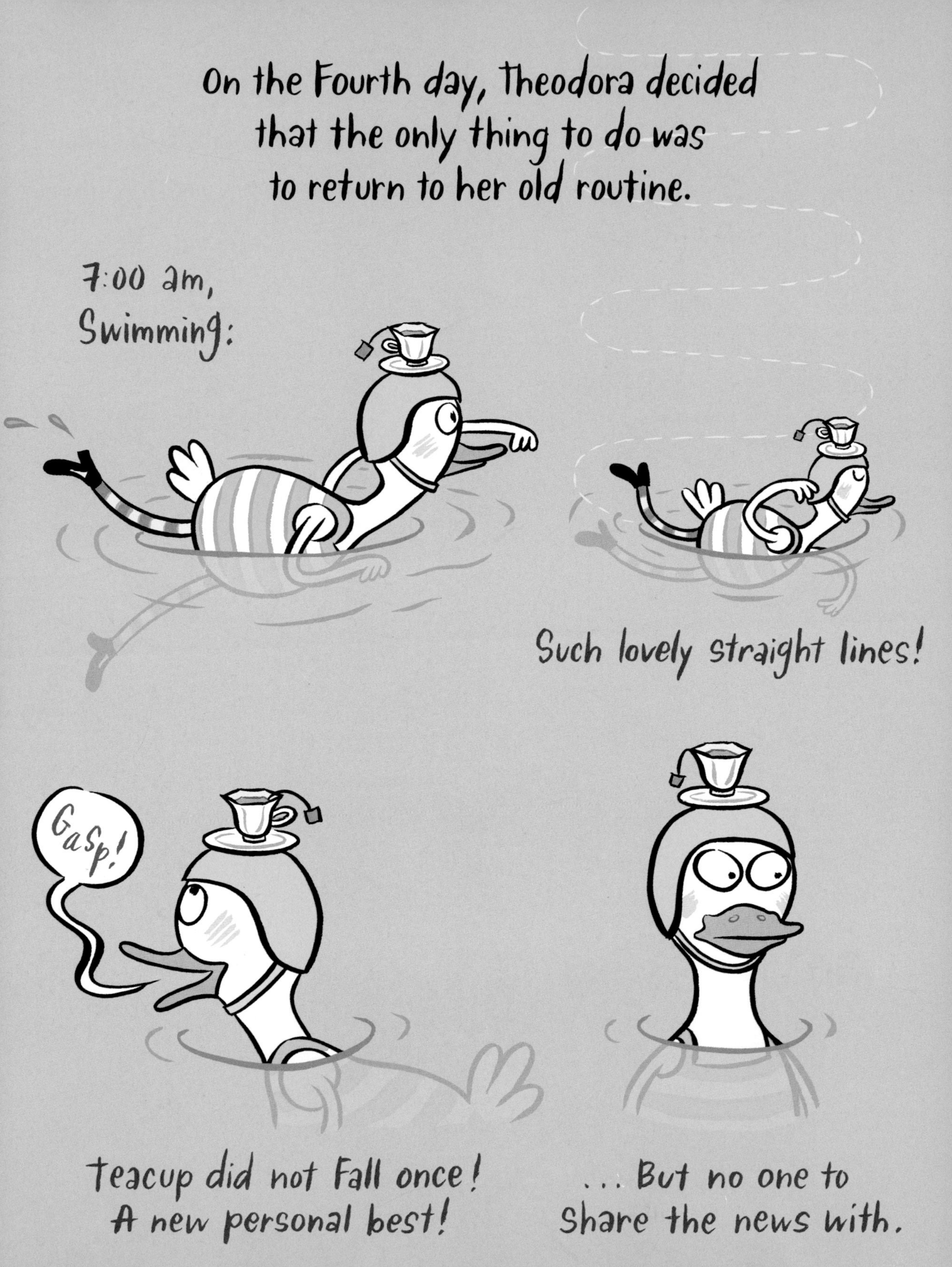
On the Fourth day, Theodora decided that the only thing to do was to return to her old routine.
7:00 am, Swimming:
Such lovely straight lines!
Gasp!
teacup did not Fall once! A new personal best!
... But no one to share the news with.

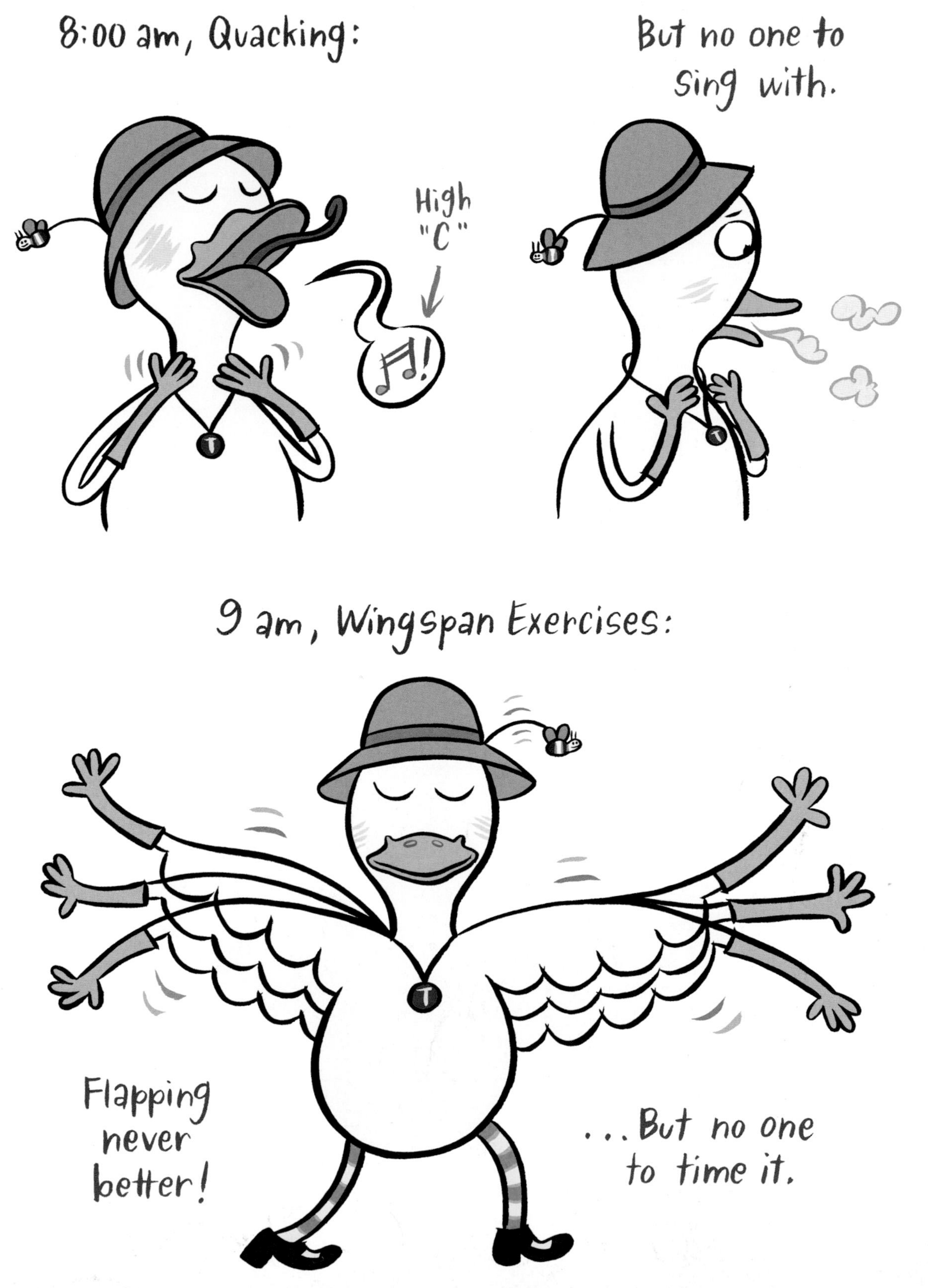

8:00 am, Quacking:
High "C"
But no one to sing with.
9 am, Wingspan Exercises:
Flapping never better!
...But no one to time it.

Then it was time for errands. First she went to see Gabe for her groceries.

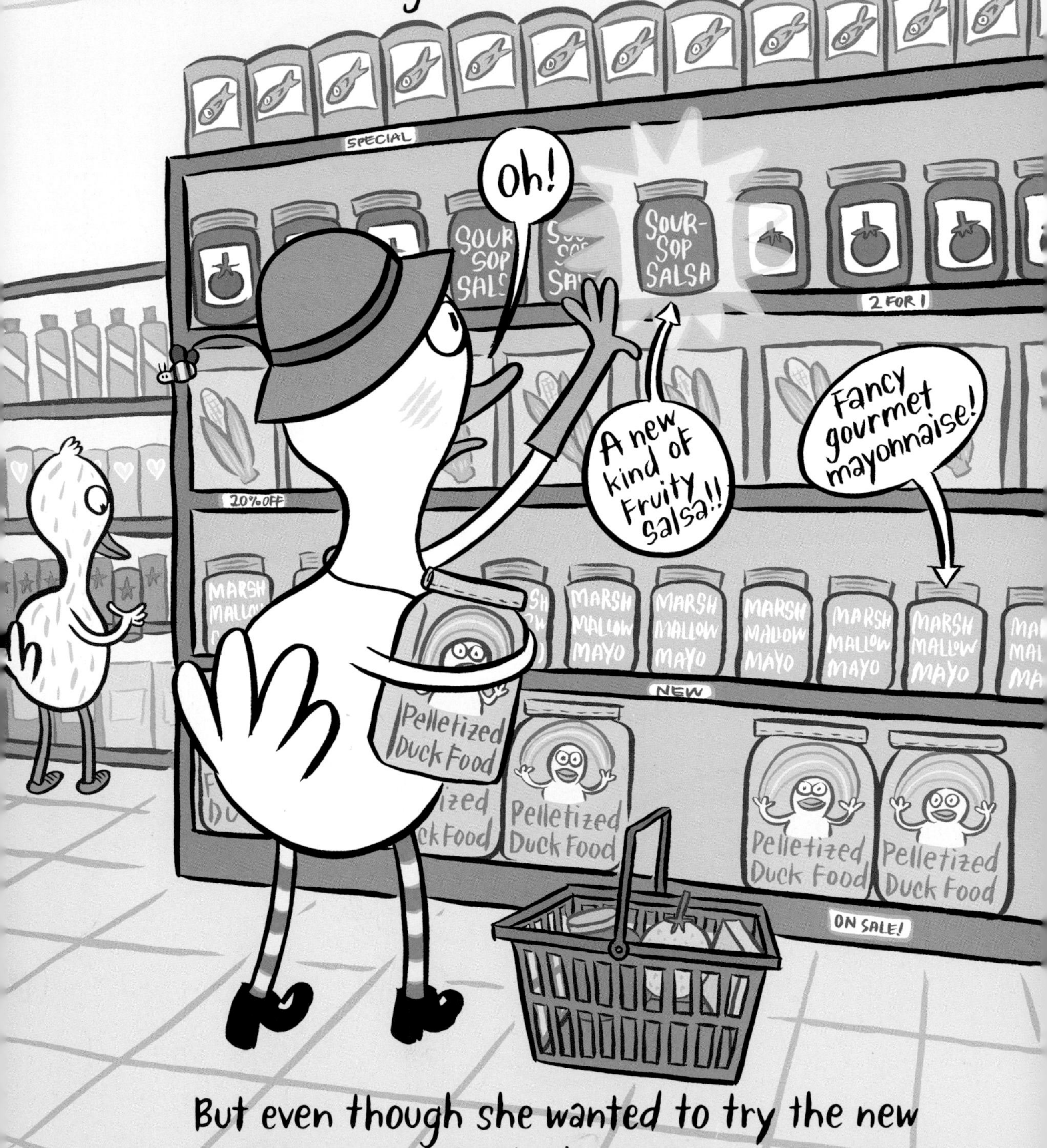

SPECIAL
Oh!
SOUR-SOP SALSA
2 FOR 1
A new kind of fruity salsa!!
Fancy gourmet mayonnaise!
20% OFF
MARSH MALLOW MAYO
NEW
Pelletized Duck Food
ON SALE!

But even though she wanted to try the new flavors, it wouldn't be fun to try them alone.

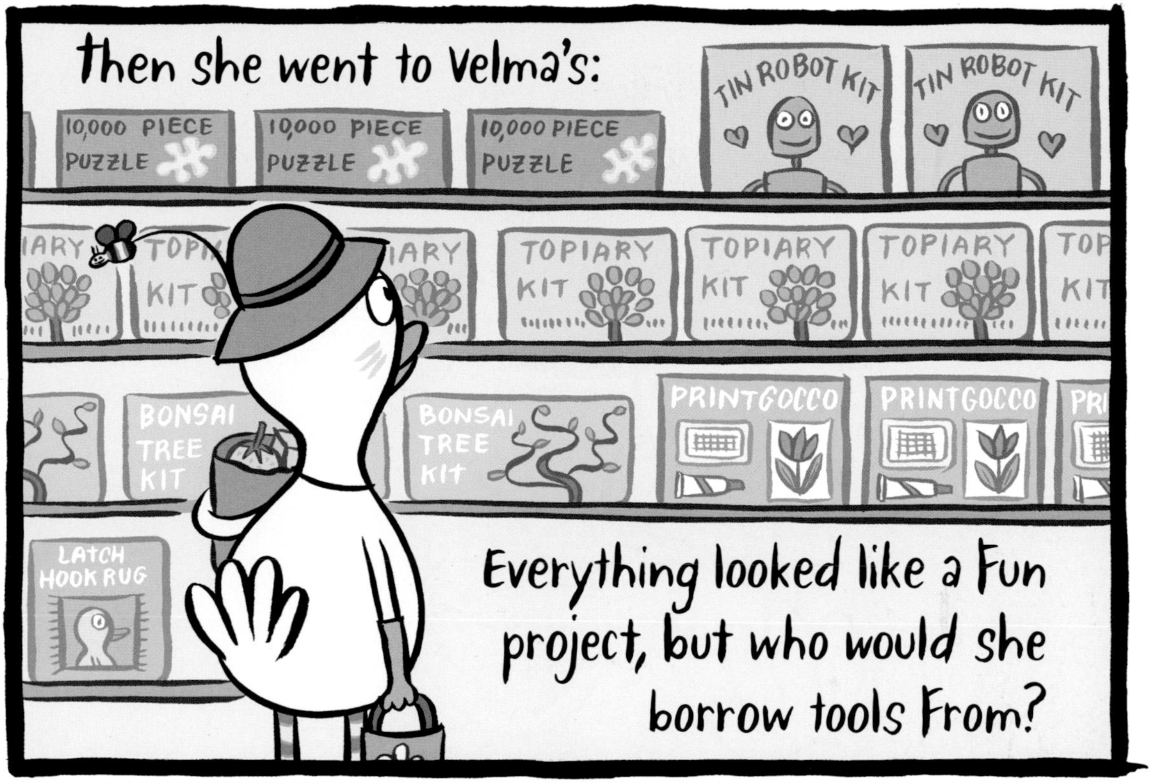
then she went to Velma's:
10,000 PIECE PUZZLE
10,000 PIECE PUZZLE
10,000 PIECE PUZZLE
TIN ROBOT KIT
TIN ROBOT KIT
TOPIARY KIT
TOPIARY KIT
TOPIARY KIT
BONSAI TREE KIT
BONSAI TREE KIT
PRINTGOCCO
PRINTGOCCO
LATCH HOOK RUG
Everything looked like a fun project, but who would she borrow tools from?

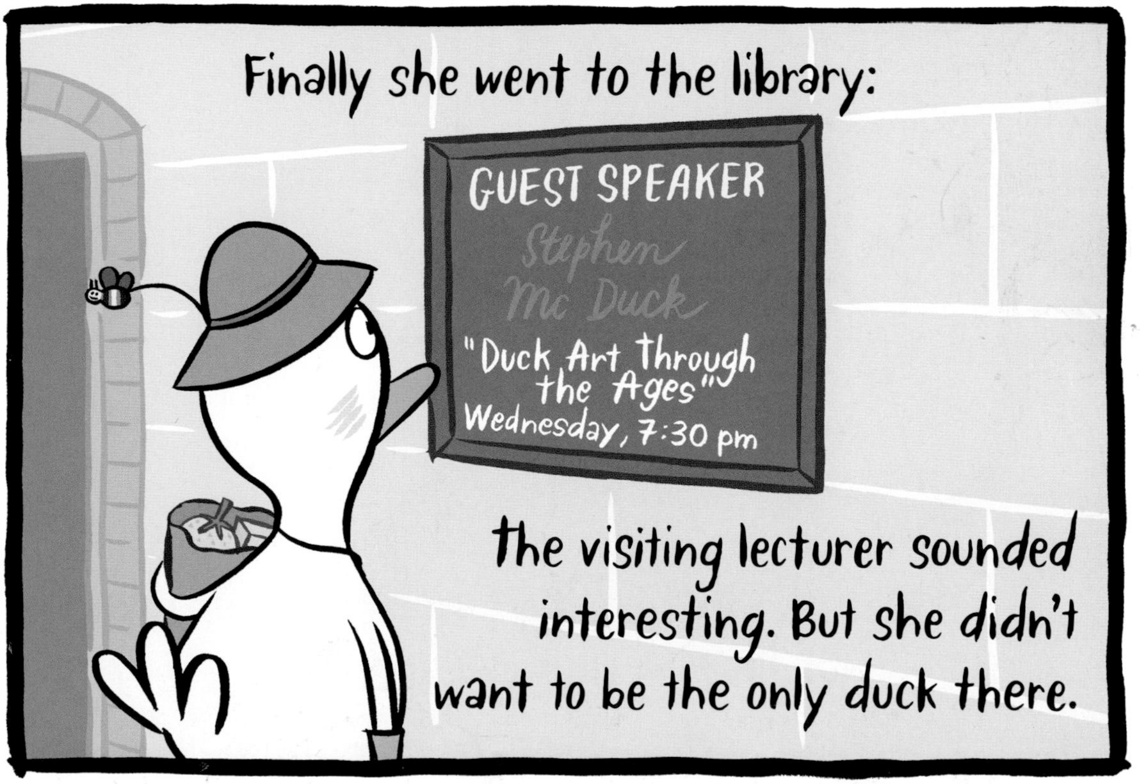
Finally she went to the library:
GUEST SPEAKER
Stephen Mc Duck
"Duck Art Through the Ages"
Wednesday, 7:30 pm
the visiting lecturer sounded interesting. But she didn't want to be the only duck there.

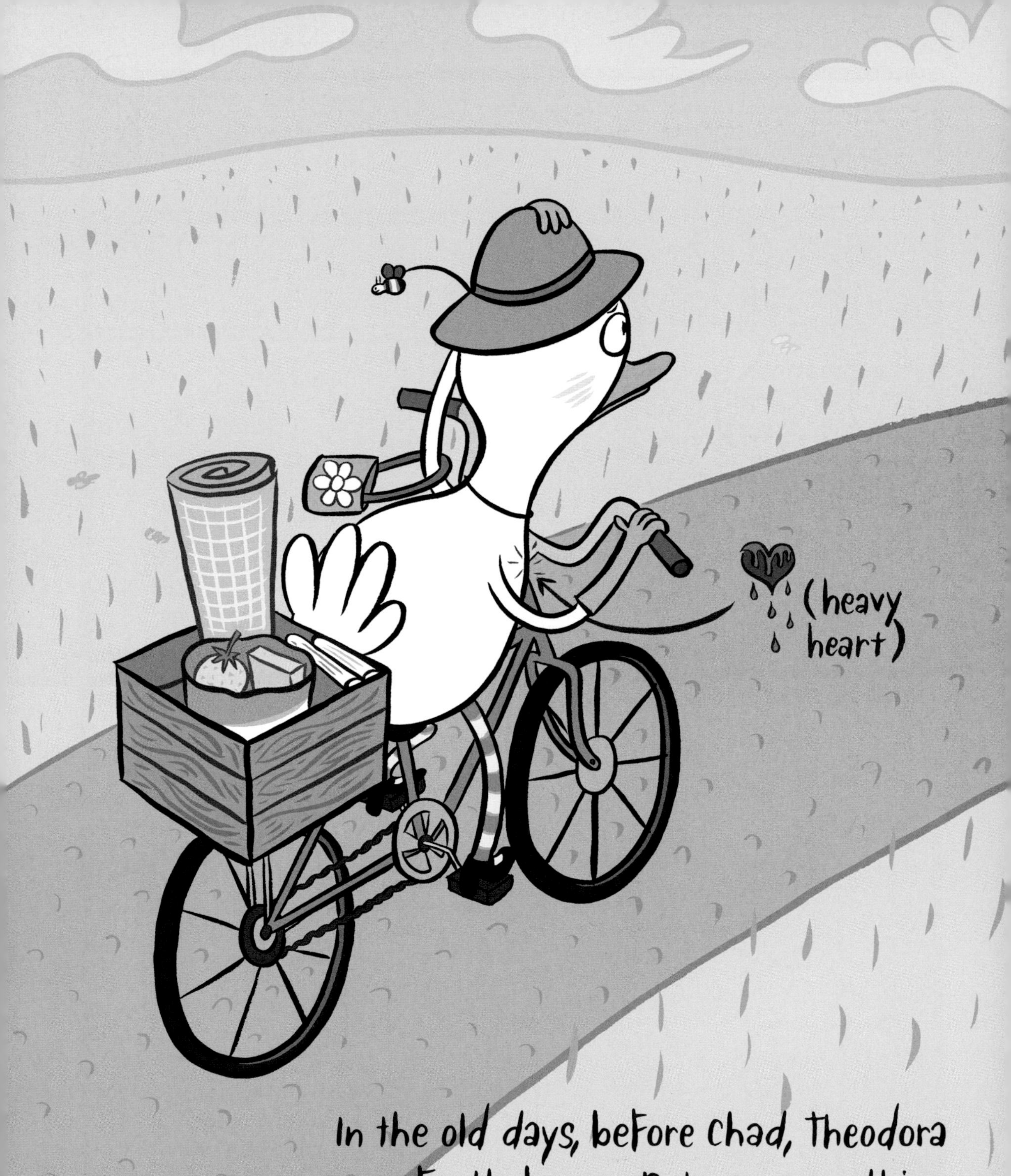
(heavy heart)

In the old days, before Chad, Theodora was perfectly happy. But now everything seemed boring without Chad to share it with.

theodora thought about calling
one of the other ducks . . .

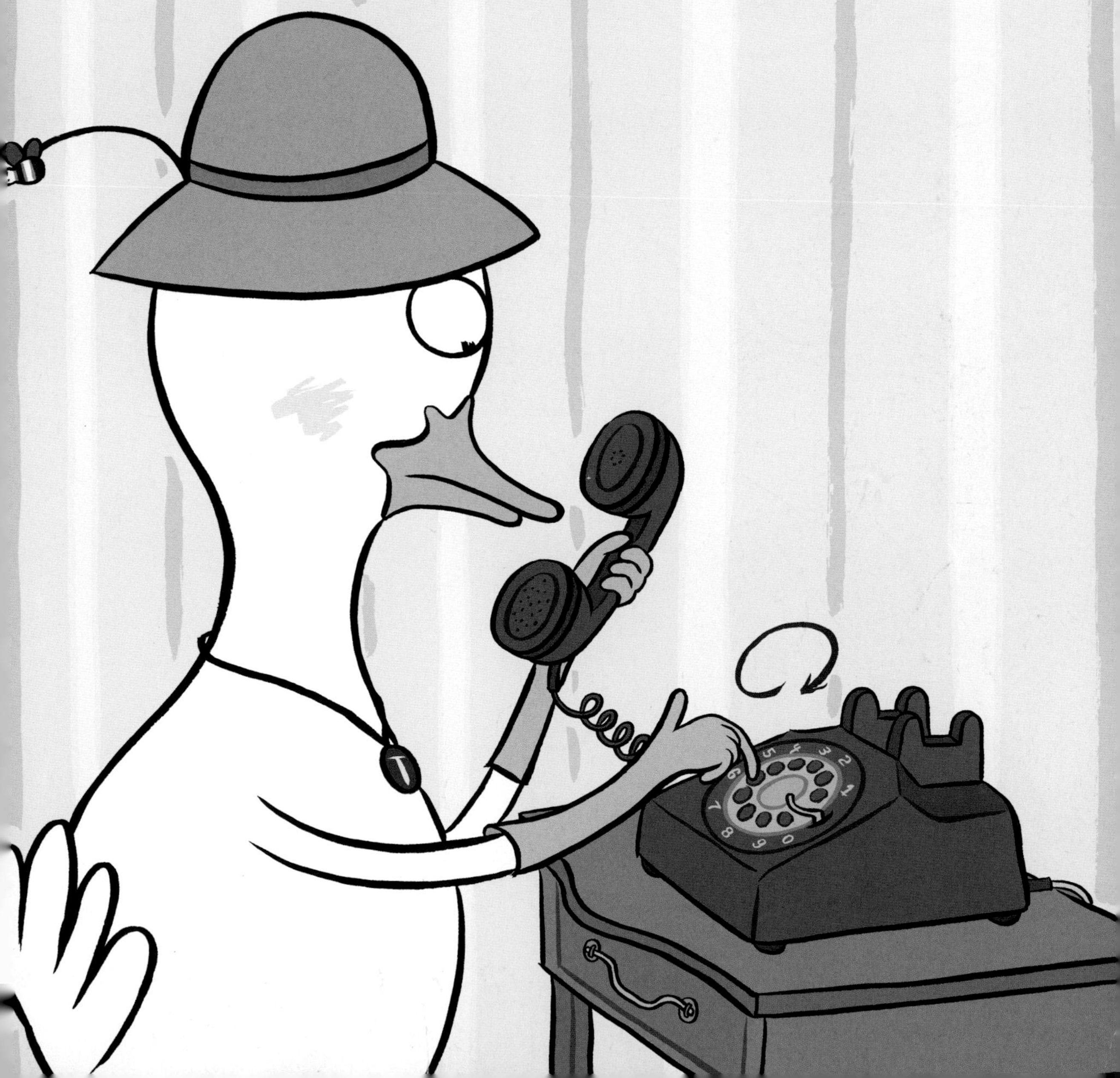

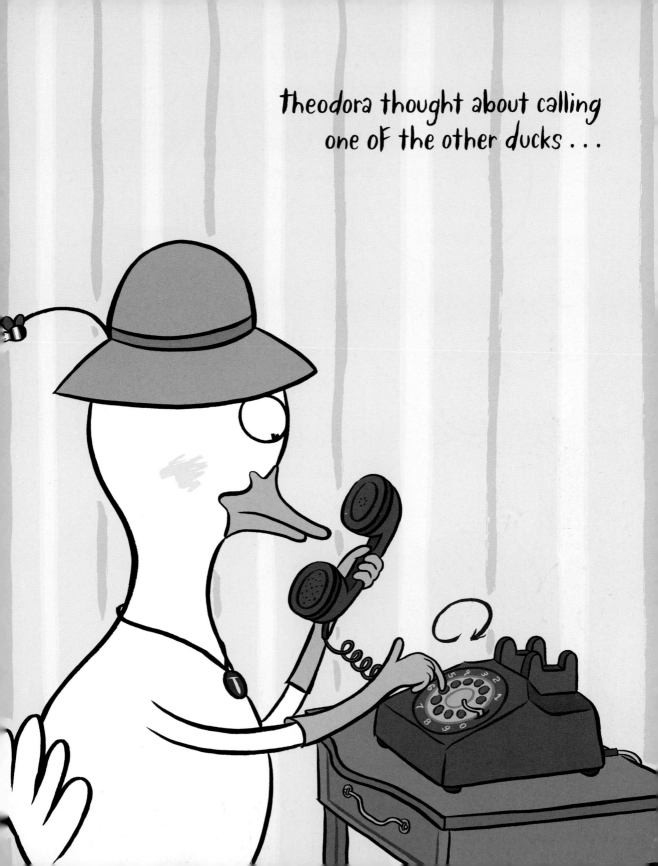

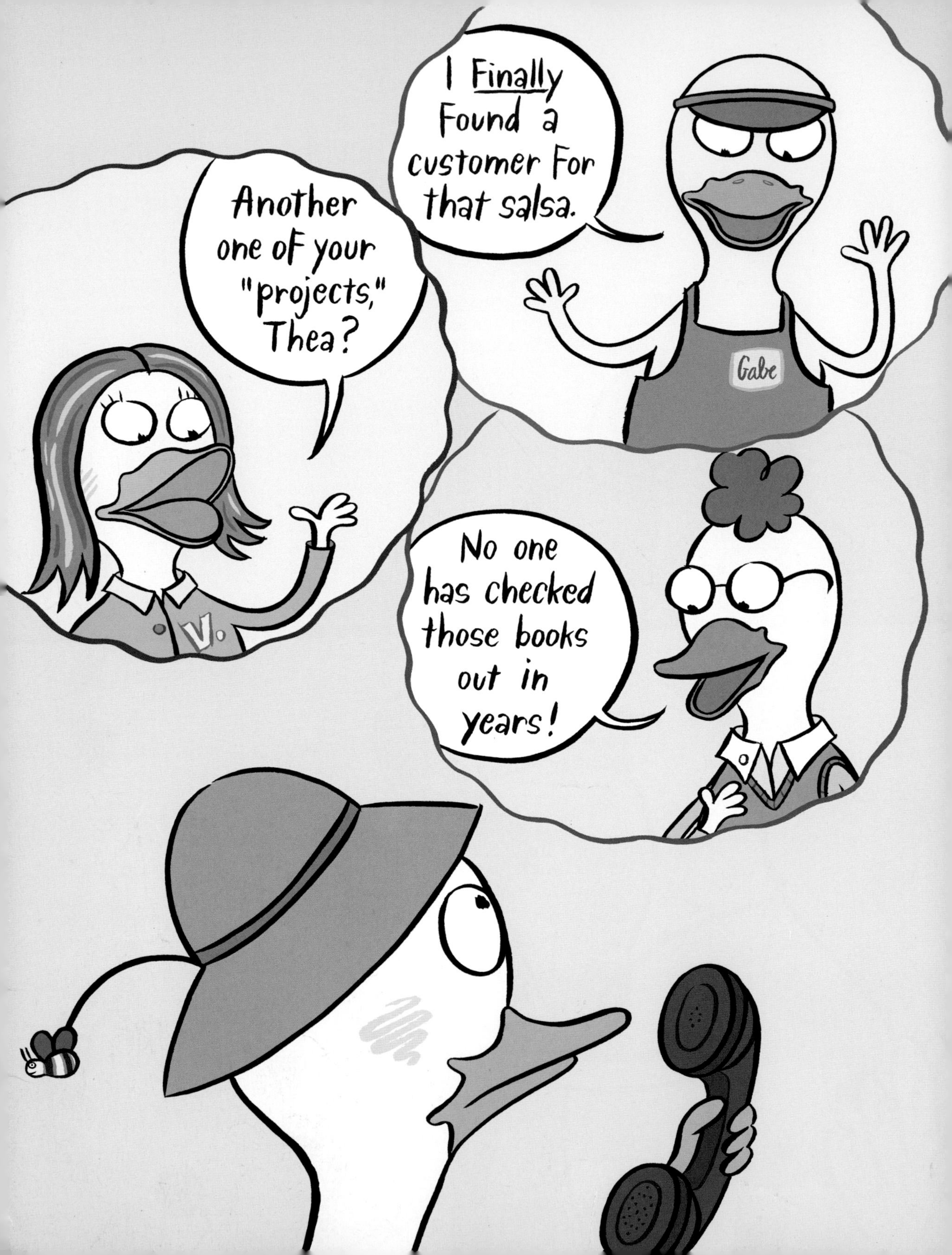
I Finally Found a customer For that salsa.
Another one of your "projects," Thea?
No one has checked those books out in years!
Gabe

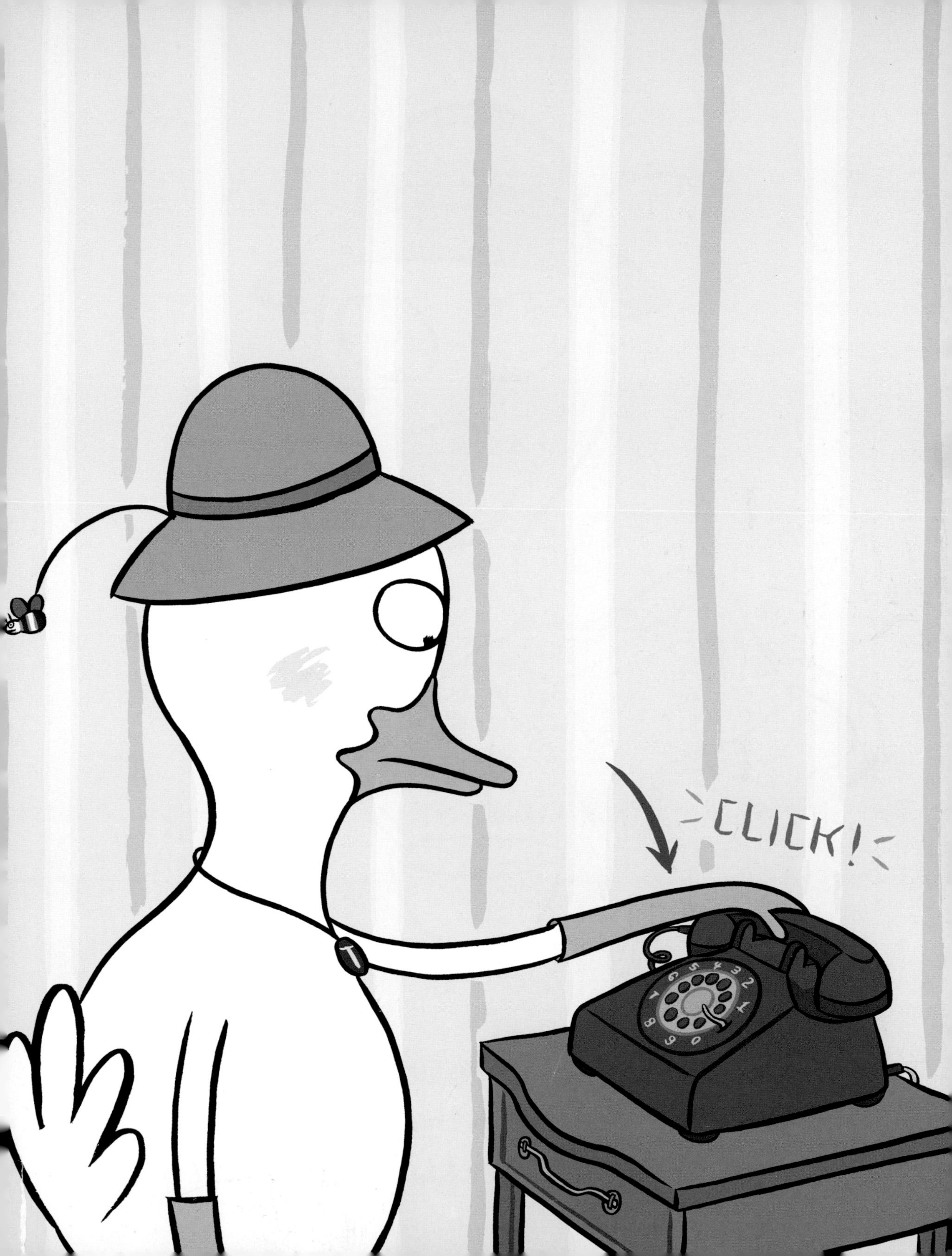
CLICK!

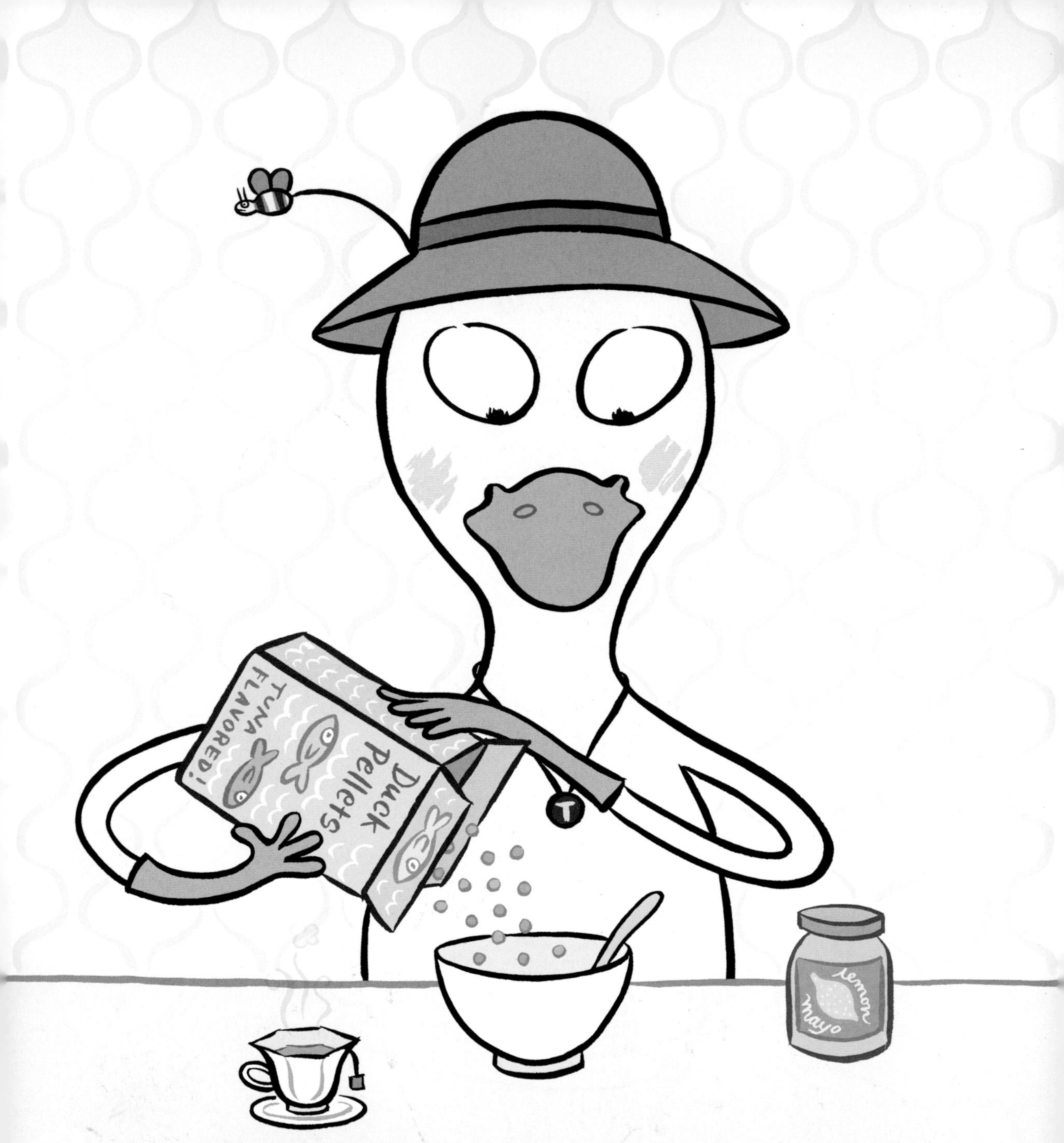
Duck Pellets
TUNA FLAVORED!
lemon mayo

As theodora prepared her supper she began to think. She did not like to think that she could be wrong, but she had never known Chad to lie.

Which could only mean one thing . . .

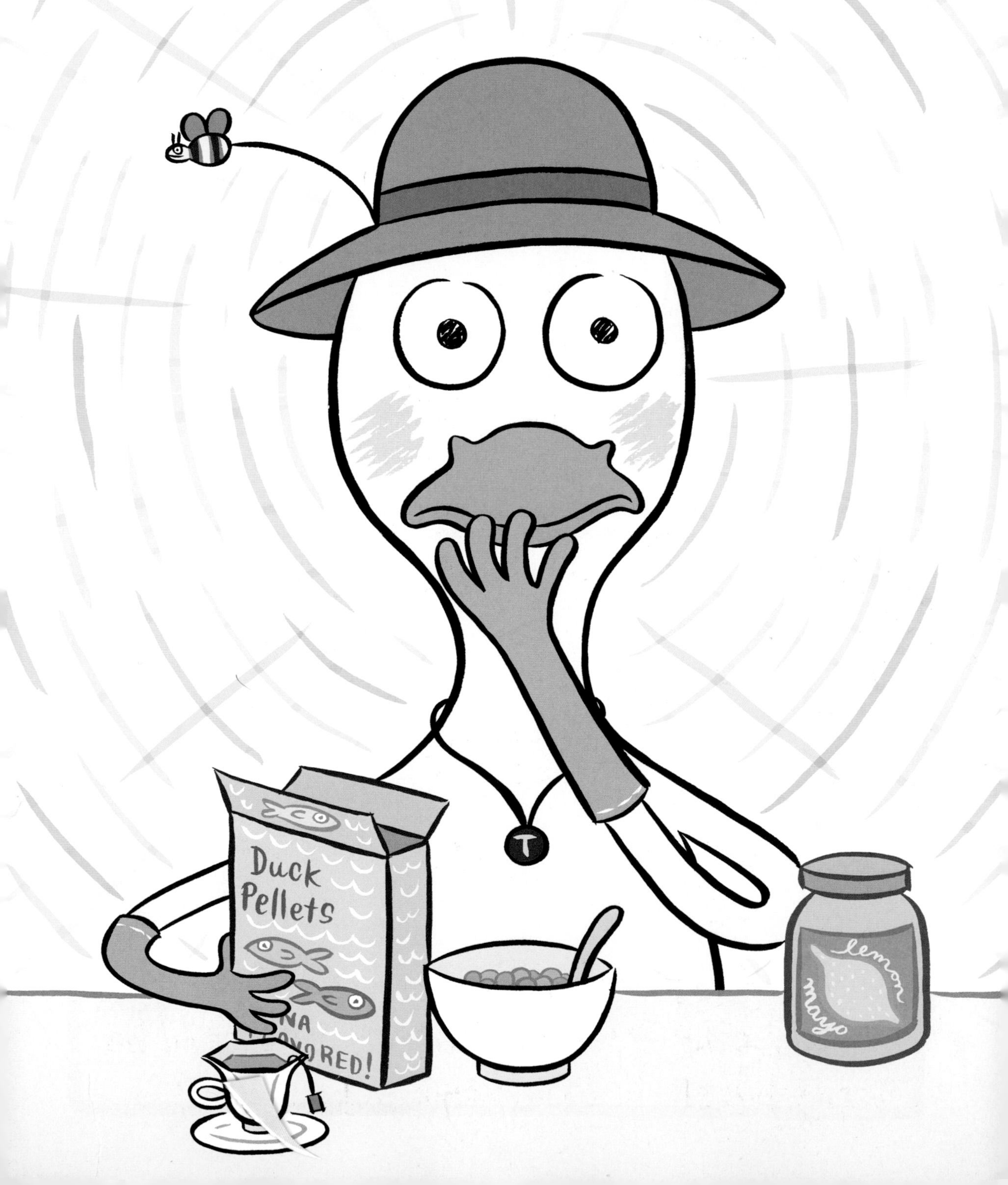
Duck
Pellets
lemon
mayo

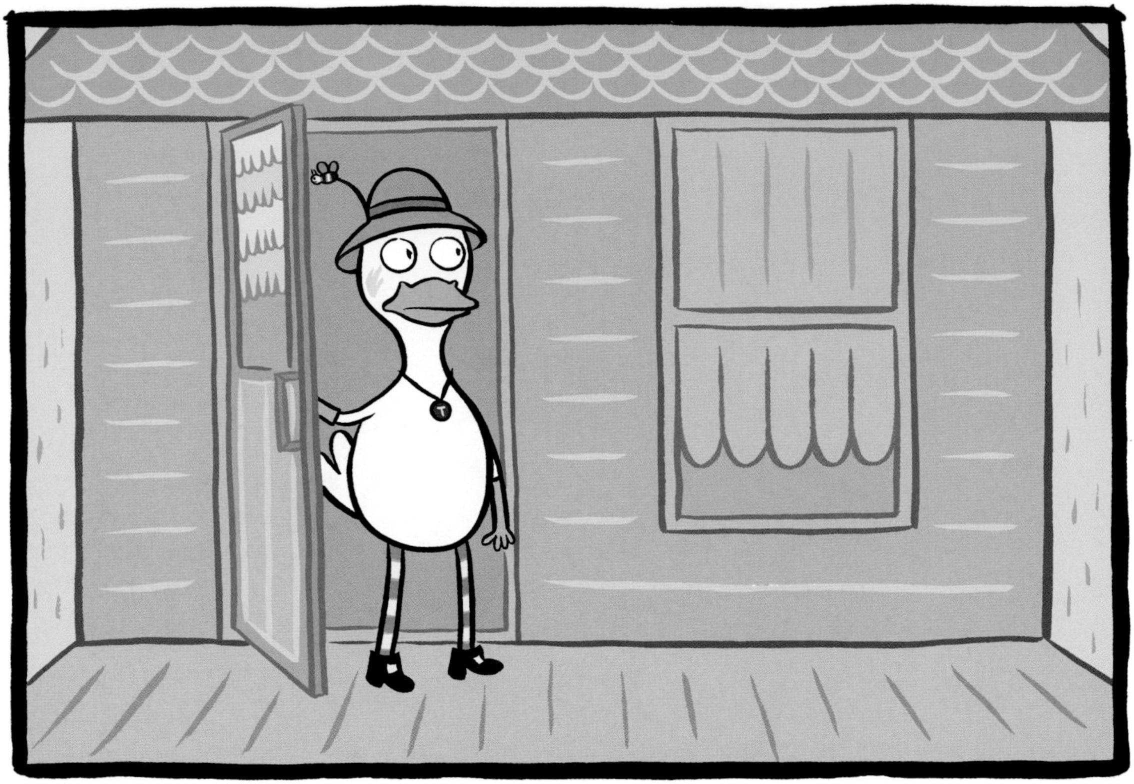

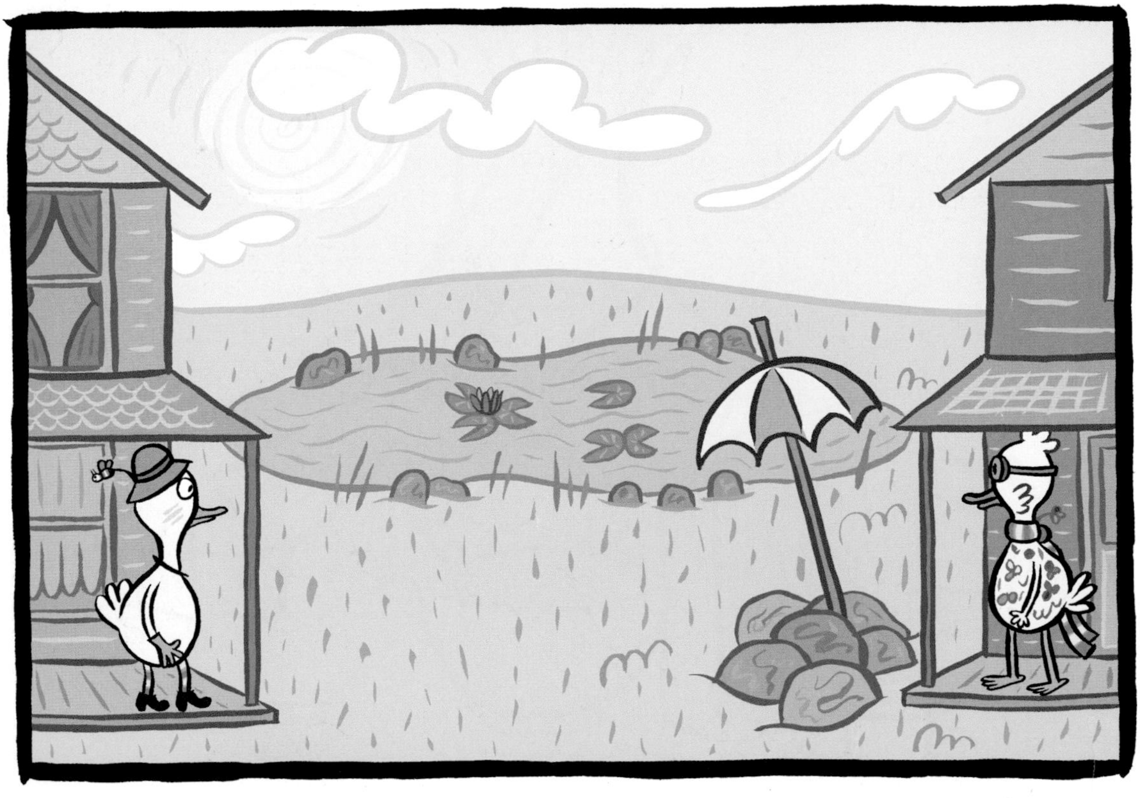

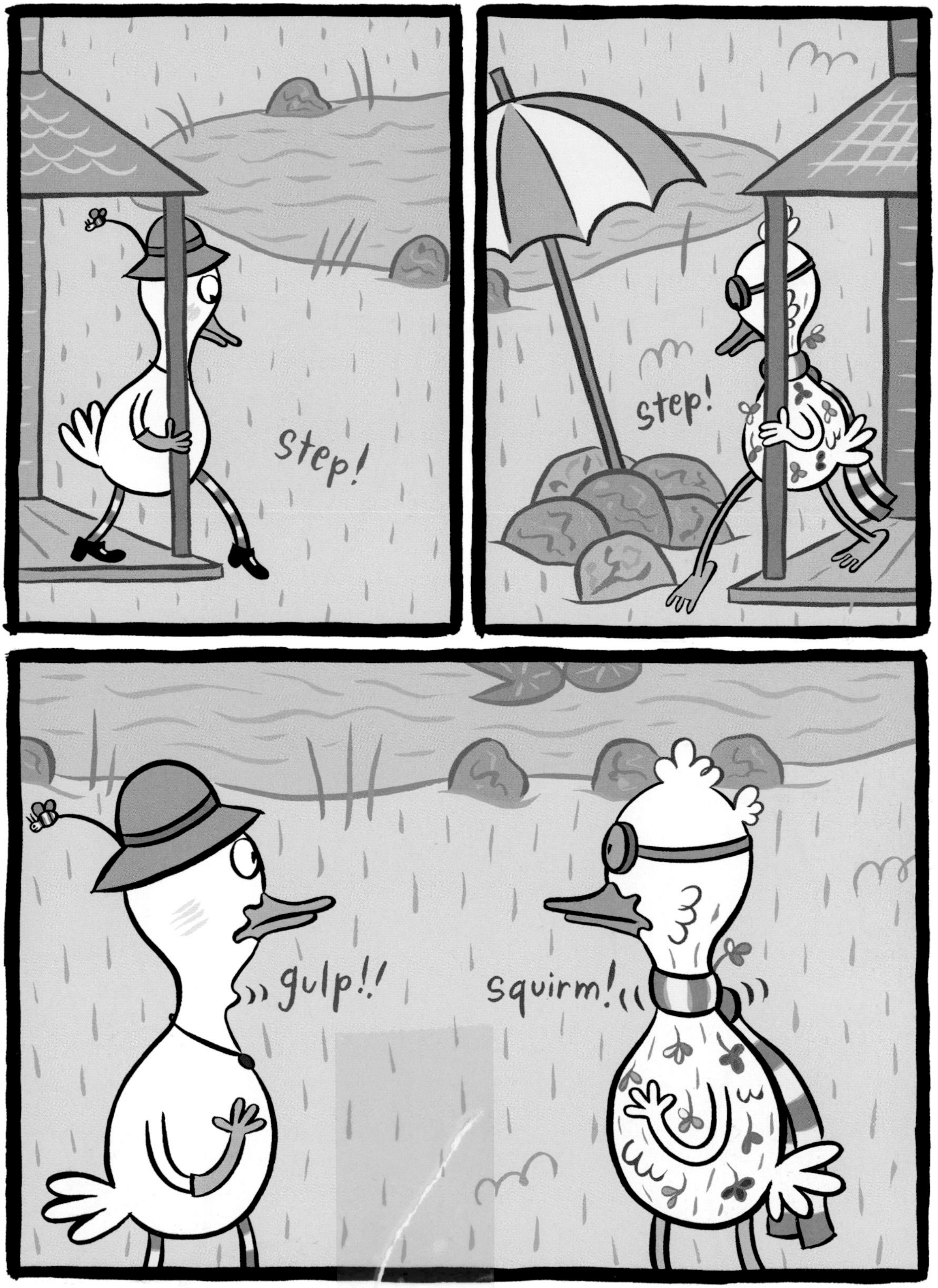
step!
step!
gulp!!
squirm!

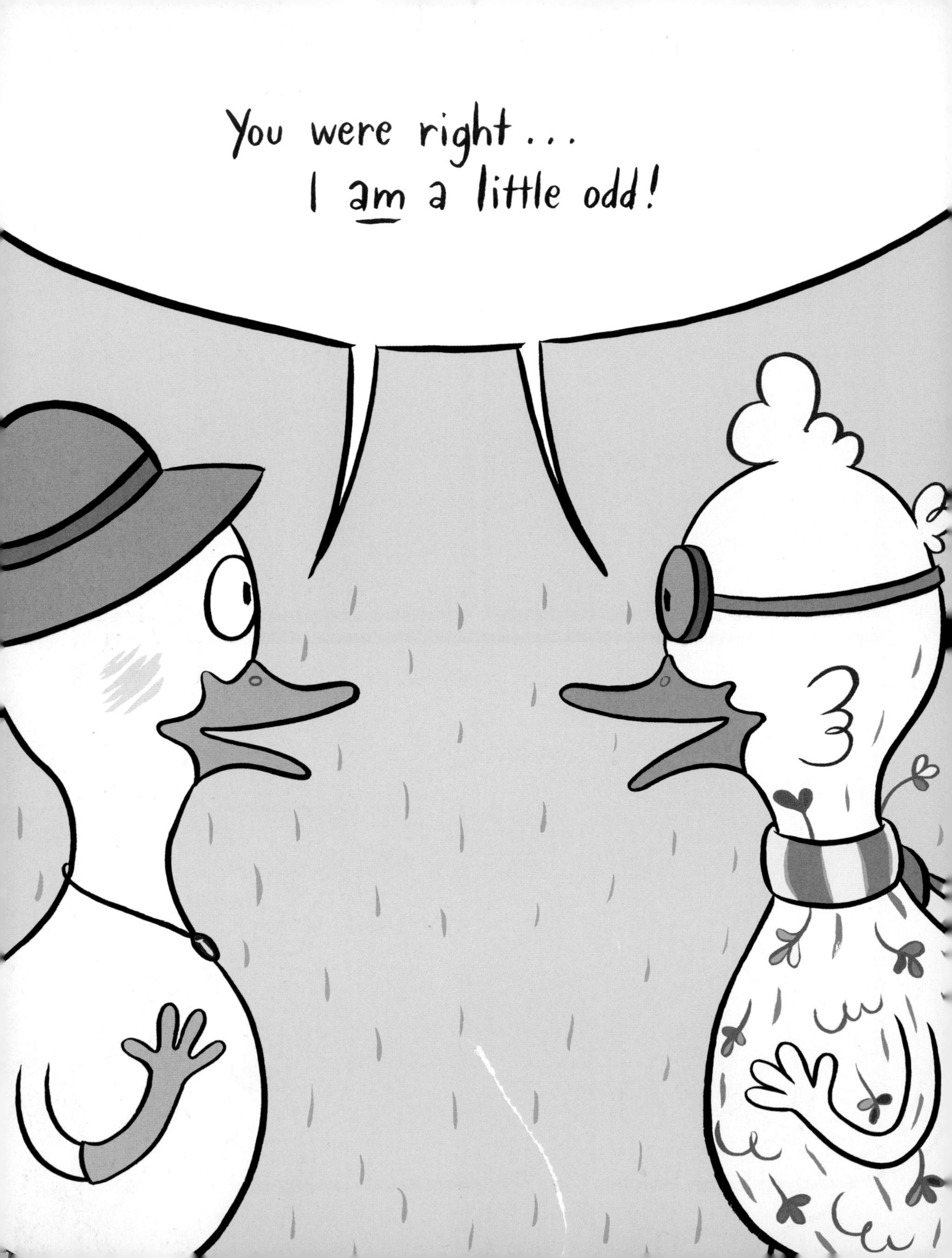
You were right . . .
I am a little odd!

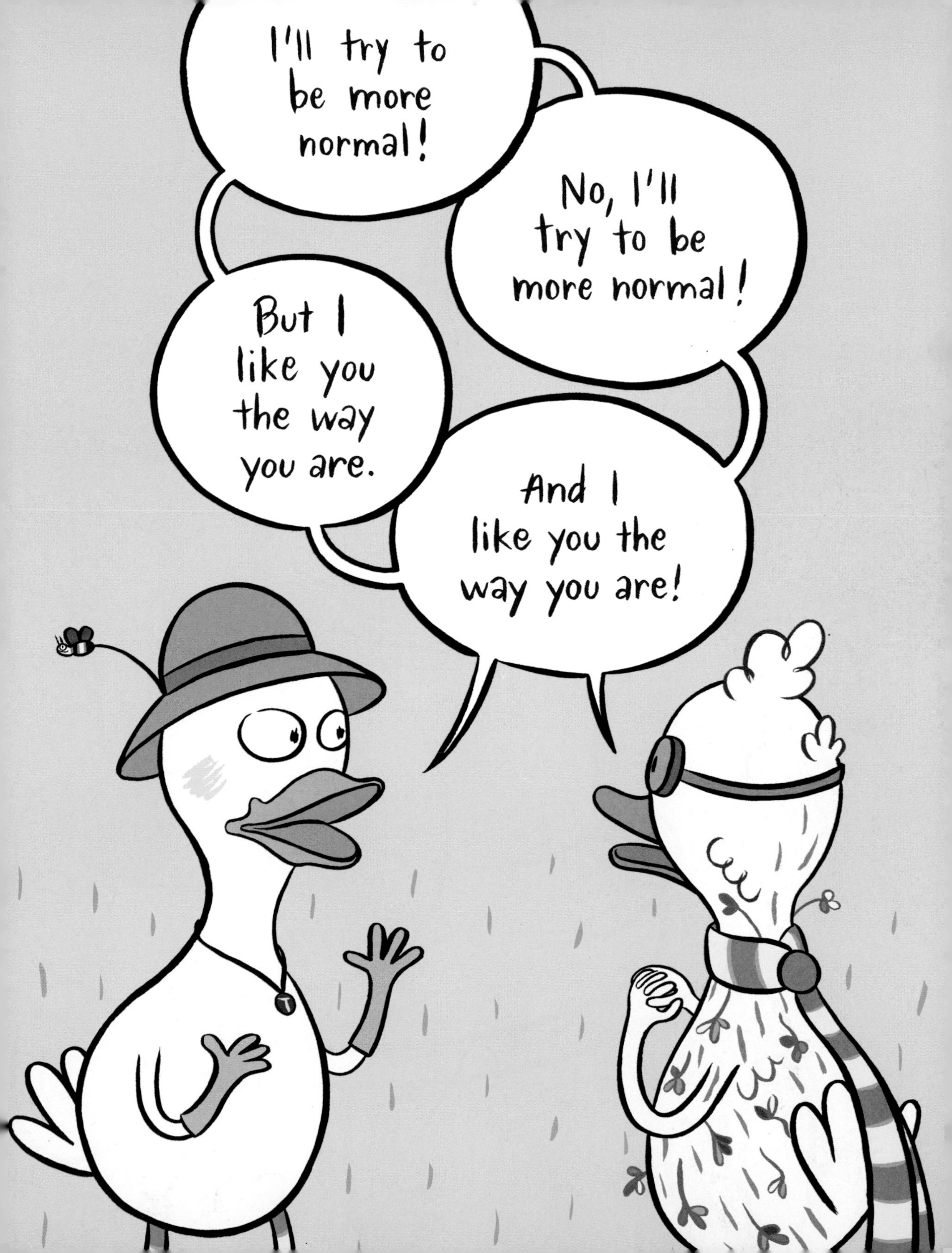
I'll try to be more normal!
No, I'll try to be more normal!
But I like you the way you are.
And I like you the way you are!

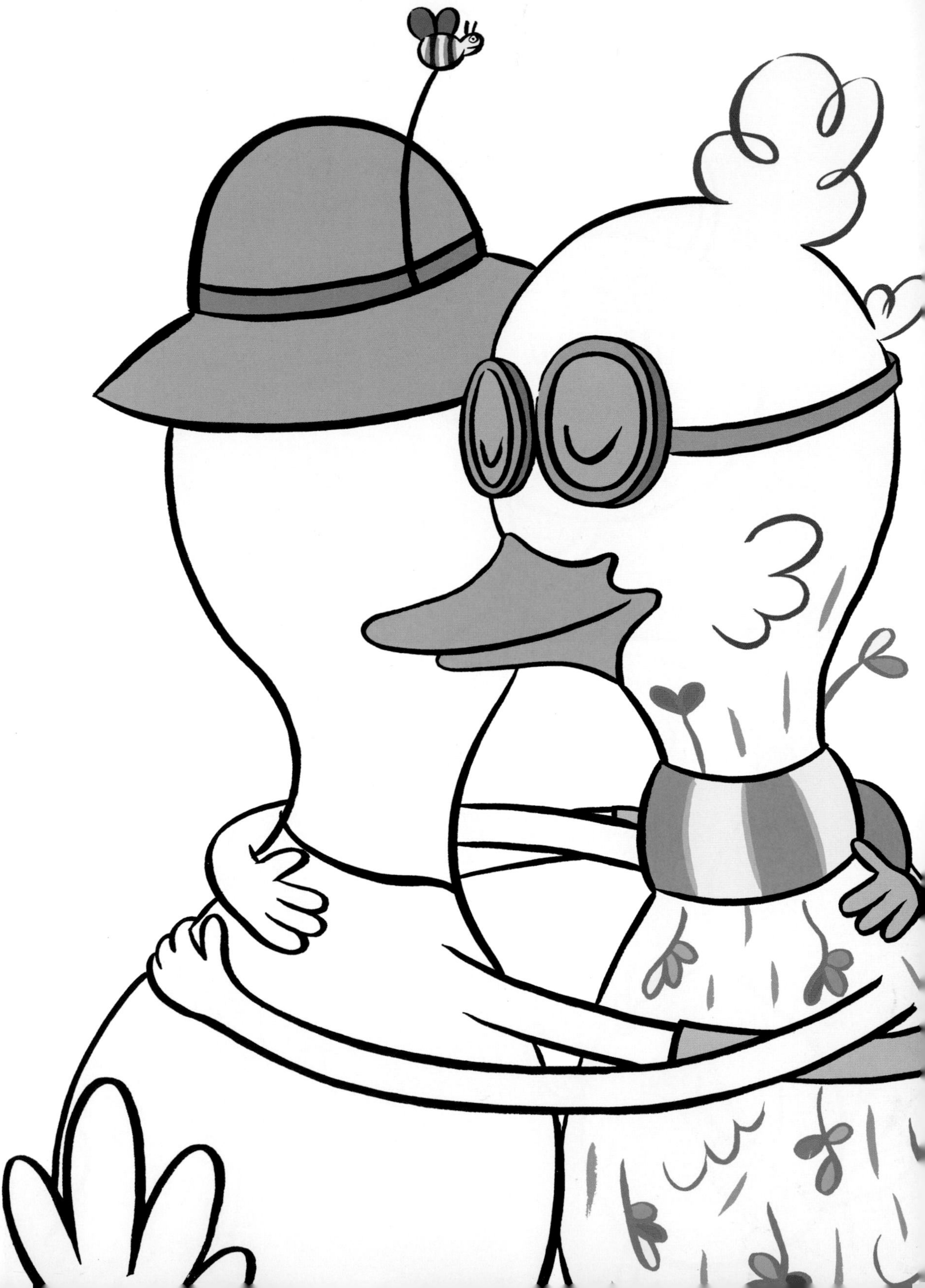

"It's not so bad to be odd,"
theodora thought . . .

"... not when you have an odd Friend."

to the oddest ducks I know: BL, MtA, and you.
—Cecil Castellucci

to my new Friends Evangeline and Joseph:
May you always be as close as Theodora and Chad.
thanks, as always, to tanya McKinnon, John Douglas,
Eddie Hemingway, and my mom.
—Sara Varon

First Second

text copyright © 2013 by Cecil Castellucci
Illustrations copyright © 2013 by Sara Varon

Published by First Second
First Second is an imprint of Roaring Brook Press,
a division of Holtzbrinck Publishing Holdings Limited Partnership
175 Fifth Avenue, New York, New York 10010
All rights reserved

Cataloging-in-Publication Data is on File at the Library of Congress
978-1-59643-557-5

First Second books are available For special promotions and premiums.
For details, contact: Director of Special Markets, Holtzbrinck Publishers.

FIRST
EDITION

First edition 2013
Book design by Colleen AF Venable
Printed in China by Toppan LeeFung Printing Ltd., Dongguan City, Guangdong Province

1 3 5 7 9 10 8 6 4 2

HOW TO DRINK TEA LIKE THEODORA!

YOU WILL NEED:
1. One pair of scissors
2. One stapler
3. One tea bag with paper label like Lipton or Twinings
4. A teacup with hot water

NOTE: If this is a library book or a borrowed book please photocopy this page and cut up the photocopy.

DIRECTIONS:
1. Cut on the solid blue and dark red lines.
2. Fold on the dotted black lines. Now you have a new label for your tea bag!
3. Staple the new label over the existing label. You can slide the string from the tea bag through the slot you created by cutting on the dark red line, so that the string hangs out of the center of the label.
4. Put tea bag in cup and drink!

Sip!

←YOU!

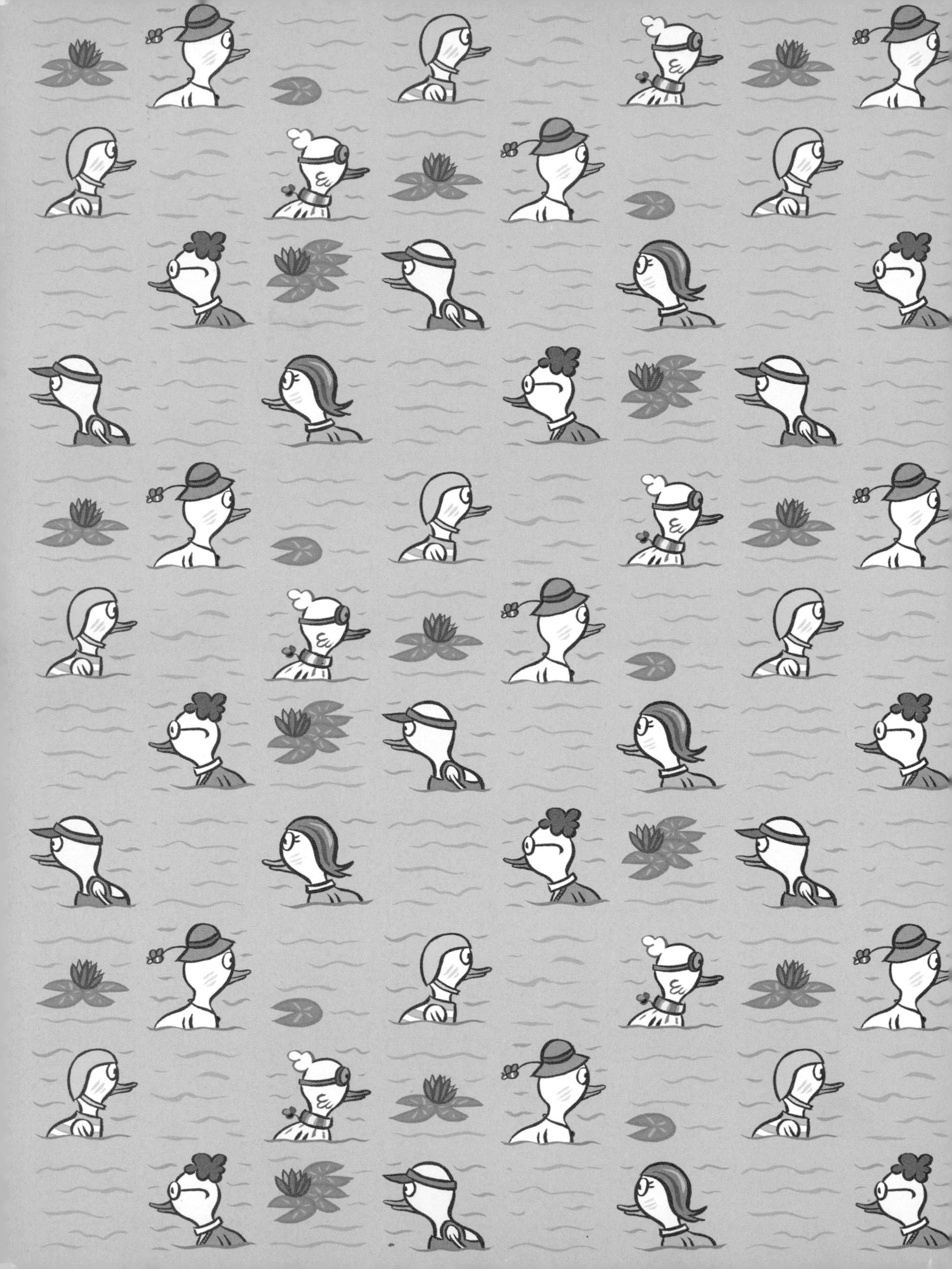

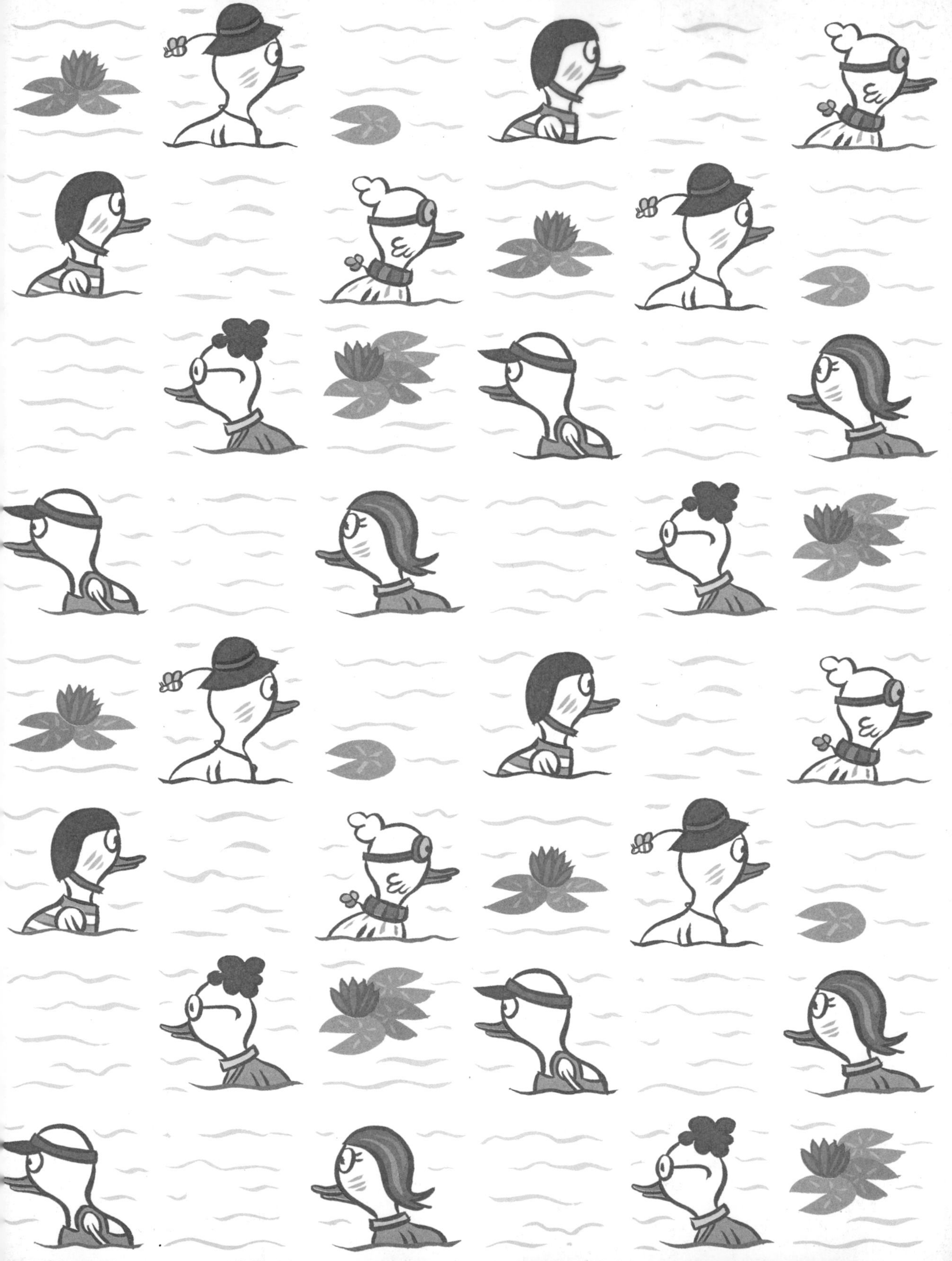

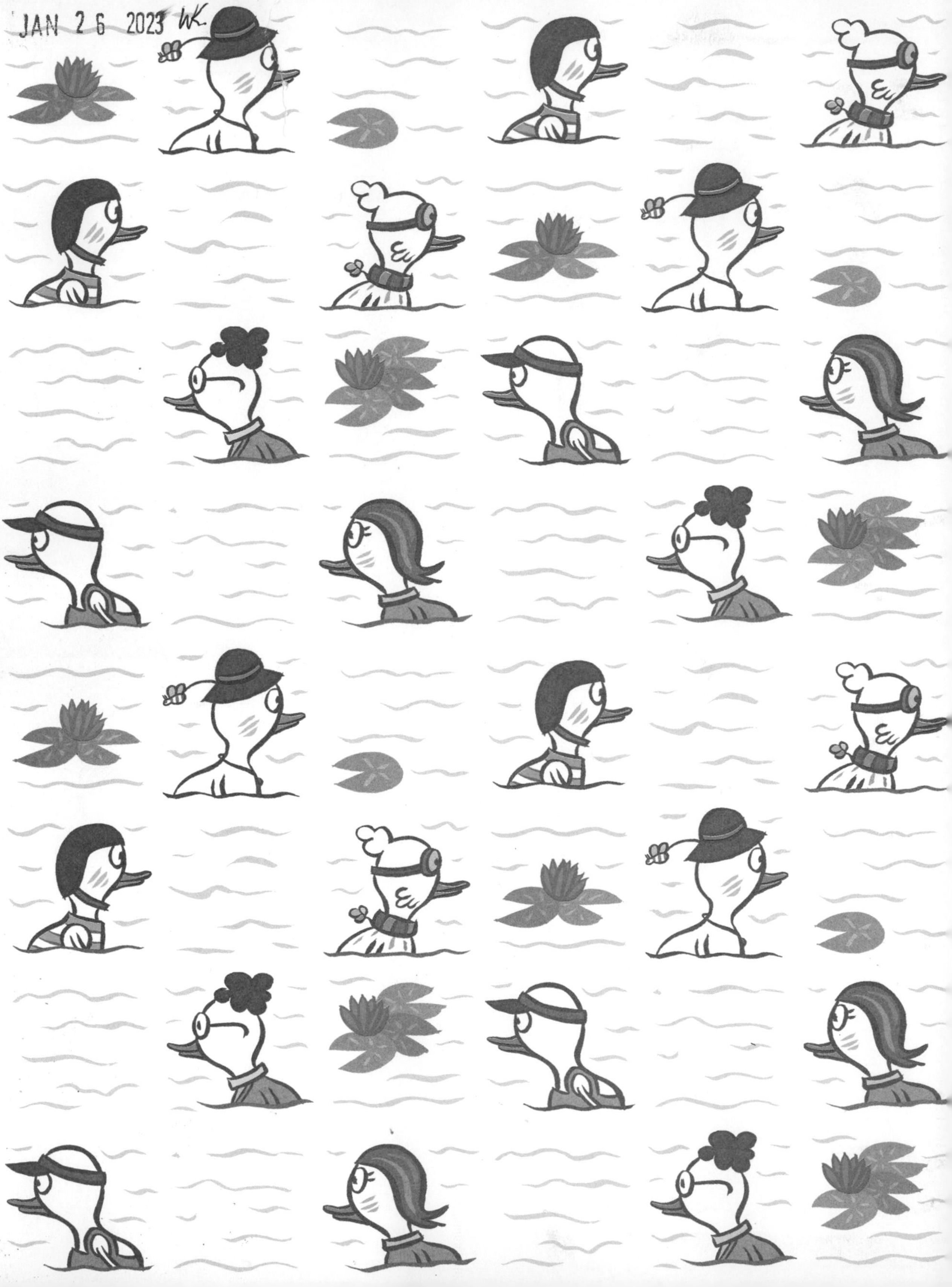